"Damn You. Why Did You Have To Come Back?"

Amy whispered.

"He's my son, too," Nick said.

"You can't mean that you intend to stay."

"Would it really be so awful having your husband home, Amy?" His gaze swept over her, and she was conscious of every part of her body that his eyes touched.

"I don't feel like I have a husband," she replied sharply, rising to her feet, desperate to escape.

"Then I've definitely stayed away too long." He spoke with a deadly softness that should have warned her. "It's time you learned what marriage really means."

Her heart raced with frantic alarm. "Nick, I don't want you," she whispered breathlessly.

"But I want you," he said softly. His eyes were as hard as diamonds. "And maybe I'm tired of wanting and never having. You're my wife. Maybe it's time I took what I want."

Dear Reader:

Welcome! You hold in your hand a Silhouette Desire—your ticket to a whole new world of reading pleasure.

A Silhouette Desire is a sensuous, contemporary romance about passions, problems and the ultimate power of love. It is about today's woman—intelligent, successful, giving—but it is also the story of a romance between two people who are strong enough to follow their own individual paths, yet strong enough to compromise, as well.

These books are written by, for and about every woman that you are—wife, mother, sister, lover, daughter, career woman. A Silhouette Desire heroine must face the same challenges, achieve the same successes, in her story as you do in your own life.

The Silhouette reader is not afraid to enjoy herself. She knows when to take things seriously and when to indulge in a fantasy world. With six books a month, Silhouette Desire strives to meet her many moods, but each book is always a compelling love story.

Make a commitment to romance—go wild with Silhouette Desire!

Best,

Isabel Swift
Senior Editor & Editorial Coordinator

ANN MAJOR
Passion's Child

Silhouette Desire

Published by Silhouette Books New York

America's Publisher of Contemporary Romance

SILHOUETTE BOOKS
300 East 42nd St., New York, N.Y. 10017

ISBN: 0-373-05445-9

First Silhouette Books printing September 1988

Printed in the U.S.A.

A Note from Ann Major:

What matters to me are the cherished people in my life—most of all my husband and my three children. When I conceived my Children of Destiny trilogy, the thoughts of family and love were uppermost in my mind.

I was born and raised in south Texas, and I've always loved our vast desolate lands that seem to stretch forever beneath blue skies. I grew up on stories of the legendary men who carved dynastic empires out of desert, men who fought Indians and bandits.

These books tell the stories of the Jacksons and Mac-Kays, two such pioneer ranching families whose lives were intertwined for one hundred years by friendship, greed, betrayal, and ultimately, love.

Book One is *Passion's Child*. Coming soon from Silhouette Desire are *Destiny's Child* (Book Two; an October publication) and *Night Child* (Book Three; a November publication).

Books by Ann Major

Silhouette Desire

Dream Come True #16
Meant to Be #35
Love Me Again #99
The Wrong Man #151
Golden Man #198
Beyond Love #229
In Every Stranger's Face #301
What This Passion Means #331
*Passion's Child #445

Silhouette Romance

Wild Lady #90
A Touch of Fire #150

Silhouette Special Edition

Brand of Diamonds #83
Dazzle #229
The Fairy Tale Girl #390

* Children of Destiny trilogy

This book is dedicated to my editor, Tara Hughes. She believed in this project and continued to guide me even when I lost faith.

And to Isabel Swift for her editorial help.

And to my friend Page Dinn for sharing the details of her glamorous racing experience during Antigua Race Week.

Prologue

Death hovered like a dark angel in the closed, airless room. There was no escape. For either of them.

Her shoulders stiff with fatigue, her body numb, Amy sat huddled beside her sister's bed where Lorrie lay groaning in labor. With each contraction, Lorrie's feverish hand clamped around Amy's in a bone-crushing, death vise of agony.

Through a mist of tears, Amy watched the snow outside blowing in the field between the trees. Oh, where was Dr. Pierce? Was he really making a house call to treat an injured fisherman as his loyal nurse had sworn, a bit too fervently, hours ago? Or was he comfortably ensconced on one of the frayed red leather stools at Big John's Tavern, getting himself stumbling drunk, his frequent condition by this time most Saturday afternoons? Or was his battered Fiat stalled on the side of some bleak highway in the snow?

An icy wind swept off the Pacific, up the high, ragged-edged, barren cliffs and moaned in the forlorn grove of stunted trees outside the window of the tiny hospital.

Inside the small building, Amy bit her lip, almost welcoming the suffering as Lorrie's fingers cut into her own again. The pain in Amy's bruised and swollen hands seemed little enough compared to what Lorrie was going through— little enough since everything that had happened to Lorrie was Amy's fault.

And Nick's. One couldn't very well forget that there was always a man responsible for every baby born. Nick had taken his pleasure, and sixteen-year-old Lorrie had been left with months of nausea and waiting, with a clumsy, thickening figure, and now with this hellish pain.

Amy would hate Nicholas Browning till the day she died for what he had done to her little sister. If only they'd never met him. If only they hadn't both been foolish enough to fall in love with him.

Amy's stricken gaze flickered fearfully to Lorrie. Her still face was translucently pale. Purple shadows lay beneath her eyes. Wet gossamer strands of inky-dark hair were glued to her bloodless cheeks.

As Amy gently brushed her sister's matted hair away from her hot sticky face, Lorrie whimpered pitifully.

"Amy! Oh, Amy, it hurts!" she sobbed. "It hurts!" She tightened her grip on Amy's wrist and pulled her closer. Lorrie's eyes were wild and glazed. "Amy, am I dying?"

Amy suppressed a shudder of sheer terror. "Of course not, darling. I'm here, and I'm going to take care of you and the baby."

"How?" came a threadlike whisper.

The single word echoed in Amy's heart. "If it's the last thing I do, I'll finish school and find a way to make enough money to support us all. I promise you."

"Oh, I—I wish I was like you—brave and strong, but ever since Mama died, I've been scared of just about everything. Like now," Lorrie whispered.

Amy couldn't bear looking into her sister's terrified eyes. "Hush, darling," she murmured in a low, strangled tone.

The trees outside nearly bent in two. Snow began to swirl.

Amy was wondering why she'd ever thought this god-forsaken fishing village clinging to the ocean's edge in northern California was a haven. It seemed a hellish prison now. But six months ago, when she'd been afraid Lorrie might do something desperate if she didn't get her out of L.A., Amy had convinced Lorrie that the only solution to their problem was for them to switch identities and come here, for Lorrie to have her baby in secrecy and give it to Amy to raise. Thus Amy had bleached her own black hair platinum blonde, the same shade as Lorrie's, and Lorrie had dyed hers black. They had masqueraded as each other. When they returned to L.A. after the baby's birth, Amy, not Lorrie, would claim the child as her own and raise it.

It had been a nightmare hiding here; a nightmare keeping Lorrie from going crazy with boredom and doing something desperate again; a nightmare evading the townspeople's prying curiosity. There was one nurse who'd somehow figured out the truth, and Amy worried about Nick tracing them here and charming the nurse into confiding in him what she knew.

Lorrie's frail body tensed in a rigor of pain, and she let out a low wailing scream that seemed to be wrenched from the depths of misery. For a moment Amy was so frightened that the breath went out of her lungs with a gasp. Then she felt her bruised hand crushed even harder.

How long did it take for a baby to come? It seemed to Amy that Lorrie had been lying in that bed for days rather than hours with beads of perspiration soaking her dull black hair as she writhed.

Amy felt for Lorrie's pulse. It seemed weak and fluttery, and Amy didn't like the way her sister had begun to lie listlessly between the pains. Her face was as gray as the winter sky outside, and breathing was growing fainter. She was losing what strength she had.

If the doctor didn't come... If the baby wasn't born soon...

The blood was thudding in Amy's ears so loudly she could hardly think. Something had to be done, and quickly.

Carefully, Amy disengaged Lorrie's fingers from her wrist and made a dash toward the door. Just as she reached it, Dr. Pierce opened it and stepped inside. The nurse, who was aware of Amy's anxiety, came in with him, hovering beside him protectively.

He was thin and old. His body bent over like a crane's, and he moved with brittle birdlike motions.

"Where have you been?" Amy cried.

Dr. Pierce looked at her with faded blue eyes. "Trying to save a dying man."

Amy heard the sense of failure in his contrite tone and said nothing more as he moved past her to examine Lorrie.

Dear God, let him save Lorrie, Amy thought.

At last he turned and whispered a battery of orders to his nurse. "The baby's in breach position. Take her into the delivery room."

The faded eyes rested briefly on Amy, but she was too numb for her mind to frame a question.

Lorrie's lips quivered as she was wheeled away from Amy, but when Amy tried to follow the stretcher, the nurse gently restrained her.

Alone, Amy sank into a chair and covered her face with her hands in despair as she listened to her sister's muffled screams coming from inside the delivery room.

It seemed to Amy that she was outside the delivery room for an eternity, keeping her silent vigil, praying feverishly to God and chewing her lip until it was raw.

In the awful hell of that waiting, one thought reeled through her tired mind. If Lorrie and the baby lived, no matter how desperate Amy might become, no matter how rich he was, she would never ask Nicholas Browning for help. She would protect Lorrie and the baby from him with her own life if necessary.

Once Amy had loved him, but he had broken her heart and turned her love to desperate hate. He had nearly destroyed her sister.

Amy knew it would be hard raising a child alone, without a father, but she was determined to succeed.

She was just as determined to hate Nicholas Browning until the day she died.

One

Damn! Nick had known Amy was trouble from the first minute he'd laid eyes on her seven years ago. She was still trouble, and she always would be.

Nicholas Browning was standing in his darkened office that overlooked the marina. He stood alone, a golden colossus of a man, staring unseeingly out the floor-to-ceiling windows at the purple sky and the gray froth of wind-whipped waves on San Franciso Bay. His black mood mirrored the turbulence of the weather outside.

Although he'd shut his door, the faint sounds of Christmas music and his staff's laughter filtered into the room.

Nick was president of South Sails, a world-famous sail loft owned by his cousin, Sebastian Jacobs. Nick's office was extravagantly decorated. Sumptuous red Persian carpets lay over gleaming parquet floors. Leather chairs and sofas surrounded his immense desk. Twin Chinese statues of apple-green jade guarded the doors. It was an office meant to impress, and it did. The man to whom it belonged was rich, successful, and proud of it.

At twenty-nine Nick was equally proud of his accomplishments. Against one wall his sailing trophies gleamed from glass shelves—two Olympic silver medals in the Sailing class and his three trophies for J-24 championships occupied positions of prominence. Above them were framed photographs of several twelve-meter yachts and their colorful spinnakers. The largest picture was of Nick, at the helm of *America's Lady*, Sebastian's challenger in the last America's Cup campaign.

Nick loved sailboats and he loved racing them. He liked designing and manufacturing sails and he prided himself in being the best at everything he did. Most men with an all-consuming passion for both their work and their play were happy men.

But he had never been like most men.

Nick didn't hear the Christmas carols. He was lost in his own thoughts. He remained at the windows, his muscular body tense, his emotions quietly controlled.

"Damn!" He expelled the curse in a taut whisper. How was it possible that one woman could bring him so much pain?

It was almost Christmas and, as usual, he was running away because for him the holiday season was the loneliest time of the year. Not that he was a man who ran away from many things. Not that he would have admitted his feelings to anyone.

Nicholas Browning had been born a bastard, and he'd learned a long time ago how to conceal loneliness behind a stubborn wall of defiant pride.

Nick jammed doubled fists into his trousers and watched the white yachts straining at their dock lines as the fierce winds began to whistle through their shrouds.

Everything had been so simple until Marcie brought him his mail.

Tomorrow Nick had been planning to leave for Australia to sail Sebastian's converted twelve-meter in the six-hundred-and-thirty-mile Sydney-to-Hobart Race and in its associated Southern Cross Cup Series. That was why Marcie had organized the early "bon voyage" Christmas party next door.

Nick went back to his desk and sat down in the leather chair behind it. On the smooth, varnished surface were neat stacks of checks he'd signed as well as invoices, letters, and file folders.

He switched on his Dictaphone, then abruptly turned it off again. He couldn't work. All he could think of was Amy.

Amy! Dear God! Why couldn't he forget her and accept their separation the way she had?

Because he wasn't made of ice the way she was—damn it! Because he'd married her for the right reasons, and she'd married him for the wrong ones.

His eyes strayed to the two pieces of personal correspondence that had arrived today. Inside Sebastian's Christmas card, he'd enclosed a picture of Amy sailing her catamaran with Triple. Sebastian's brief note said that Amy had sent the photo in her Christmas card to him. Amy worked for Sebastian, too, and though she had nothing to do with the South Sails operation, she was one of Sebastian's most valuable executives.

It infuriated Nick that she treated Sebastian like family while ignoring her own husband. Amy had been Nick's wife for more than five years, and never once since their separation had she willingly corresponded with him.

Why the hell did he still care? Nick picked up the picture. He would have given anything to feel indifferent toward her, but the mere sight of her laughing, upturned face sent his pulse thudding with a violent mixture of unwanted emotions.

She hadn't smiled at him like that in years! He stared at the glossy image of a slim young woman strapped into a trapeze, hiking out with only her feet against the side of the boat. A soaked, long-sleeved white T-shirt was plastered to her body. The water made it transparent so that the lines of her bikini were clearly visible. Not that Amy usually wore a bikini in public or ever wanted herself to be photographed in one. She was prim and proper to the core.

His gaze swept over her full breasts, down her flat belly, down the curving length of her brown legs. Memories of her supple body beneath his, her arms wrapped around him, her hands clinging, her soft voice crying out assailed him.

Once she'd been his touch, to caress, to love. Once he'd made her forget how improper it was for a lady to go wild in bed. Then he'd lost her—completely, irrevocably—and he still didn't know why. Maybe that was the reason he couldn't let her go.

In the picture, her long black hair flew about her neck and face in lustrous tangles. Usually she wore it primly secured at the nape of her neck in that tight little knot he detested. He remembered the perfumed scent of her hair—the silken feel of it against his cheek as it fanned out over his white pillow. The last time he'd slept with her had been two years ago. She'd come alone to San Francisco for his younger brother Jack's funeral, and when Nick had turned to her in his uncontrollable grief, she'd ended up in his bed. But the next morning she'd left him, and her determination to have nothing to do with him had seemed even stronger than before.

Why, damn it? Why?

In the photograph, Triple was at the helm—Triple who was only six years old—and the catamaran was difficult for

even a man to manage. Nick felt a surge of paternal pride as
he examined the image of his sturdy little boy. Triple's jaw
was squared with determination, every muscle in his small
body straining as he gripped the tiller and fought to control
the boat.

For all her coldness as a wife, at least Amy was a warm
and dedicated mother. Triple wasn't an easy child. He was
bold and precocious, and he had a peculiar penchant for
bringing disaster on himself by tackling tasks too difficult
for him. He'd been christened Michael John Browning.
From the crib he'd been three times as much trouble as an
ordinary child would be, and from a multitude of mischievous activities he'd derived his nickname, Triple Trouble,
which had long since been shortened to Triple.

The hastily scrawled inscription at the bottom of the picture read:

Dear Sebastian,
    This was taken right before Triple lost hold of the
tiller and we capsized. Triple got pretty mad when we
landed in the water.

Love, Amy

Nick smiled. He always got mad at himself when he made
mistakes sailing. Jack had been like that, too. Nick cut the
painful thought short. He still found it hard to accept losing Jack.

Nick forced himself to set the picture aside. There was no
use torturing himself by looking at it. He'd made a bargain
to stay out of their lives for eleven months out of the year.
But every July, Triple was his. Only July. The rest of the
year Nick tried to forget he had a family. Of course, he sent
cards and small gifts on holidays, but he'd learned he was

happier if he put Amy and Triple out of his mind and concentrated on his work.

Nick knew she didn't want him. Sometimes he wondered if she ever had. Had Amy done all of it only because he was rich and she'd been after money, dropping him when she'd seen a way to make use of Sebastian instead—and have her independence, too?

Nick picked up the Christmas card that Triple had sent and studied his son's scribbled, misspelled message once more.

All I want fro Christmas is to see yuo, Dad. Love, Triple.

Every time Nick reread the brief note, he knew that he felt the same about Triple. It was hell having a son, and yet not having him. Hell, flying to the other side of the world to race a sailboat when all he really wanted to do was spend time with Triple.

The spelling mistakes pulled at something else inside Nick. Triple had inherited dyslexia from him. His case wasn't as severe as Nick's had been. Lots of first-graders mixed up letters, but Nick knew from experience how much more difficult it was going to be for Triple to learn to read and spell. More than anything Nick wished he could be there to help him.

But that simply wasn't possible. Amy would never allow it.

Anger ripped through Nick. Triple's card was a plea for love. Only someone with a heart of stone could ignore it.

Who did she think she was? Triple was his son, too, and it was Christmas.

Nick glanced at his watch. It was nearly four. Triple was probably home already for the holidays, but Amy would still be at work.

To hell with her.

Nick reached for the telephone and punched the buttons briskly. Even though he rarely called Triple, he knew the number by heart.

"Hello..." The vibrant feminine greeting was a husky caress. The unexpected sound of Amy's voice jarred his nervous system.

She had been expecting someone, someone she obviously wanted to talk to. Was it another man?

The muscles in Nick's stomach contracted sharply at the thought.

"Hello," she repeated, still sounding friendly, though a little uncertain.

He imagined her sitting rigidly at her desk in that austere little office in her Malibu home. He had bought her that house and she'd said she hated it because it was too extravagant—like him.

She was probably wearing a suit made of stiff material buttoned tightly to her throat—something she'd bought on sale somewhere. Her hair would be pulled back in that awful little bun.

"Hello," he managed at last, the low tones of his own voice oddly strained. "It's me. Nick."

Her swift intake of breath was like a gasp of pain. She expelled his name in a rush of hostility. "Nick! How dare you—" She caught herself. It was her custom to treat him with no show of emotion.

A long, hushed silence followed. It was taking her longer than usual to gain control of herself.

"We made a bargain," she said in her coolest, most businesslike tone.

"*You* made the bargain," he ground out, fighting to hold on to his temper. "I have a right to talk to my son."

"Not by the terms of our agreement."

"Your agreement," he corrected.

"Nick, this is the best possible solution."

"For whom?" His short, brittle laugh was forced. "Just get Triple on the phone," he snapped.

Nick expected her to hang up on him. To his surprise she didn't.

"He's not here right now. Dad took him Christmas shopping a while ago."

"Why didn't you say so?"

"Because—" She broke off. "Because I don't want you calling here. Ever."

"It's Christmas. Triple sent me a card and told me he wanted to see me. I thought maybe I could stop off in L.A. tomorrow on my way to Sydney. I could see Triple for an hour or so while you're at work."

"No!"

"Did it ever occur to you that maybe it would be good for Triple if I saw him more often?

"No, Nick." Her voice was losing that prim, no-nonsense quality. She sounded vulnerable, frightened. "I won't have Triple torn between us."

"Isn't that what you're doing by forcing me to stay away from him?"

"I don't want you in my life!"

"We're talking about Triple's life."

"Nick. Please . . . No."

"Triple needs me whether you believe it or not. I'll be there tomorrow. If you don't want to see me, make sure you're not around tomorrow afternoon. That shouldn't be too hard. We all know how dedicated you are to your career and making money."

He realized how harsh he sounded. When Amy tried to boss him around, no matter how he strained to hold on to his patience, his temper always got the better of him. But he didn't want to end their conversation on a hostile note. He softened his voice. "Of course, I'd rather see you, too. We haven't seen each other since the night after Jack's funeral."

If Amy hadn't come to him then and restored his faith in the sweetness of loving, he might never have made it through the darkest hour of his life, Nick thought. His own family had stayed in Texas where the real funeral and burial services had been held.

"The night . . ." Her soft voice faded away.

He imagined her brows drawing together as an unwanted blush suffused her cheeks. She would be biting her bottom lip, too. Prim and proper Amy wouldn't like remembering the long, wanton night they'd shared.

"Are you afraid to see me?" he accused huskily. "Afraid we might end up in bed again?"

She had regained control of herself. "Why, you conceited, low-down..." She searched for a suitable insult. "Sex maniac!" she hissed.

"Thank you," he murmured, some inner demon driving him to goad her. "It was wonderful, wasn't it?"

"You are the most insufferable egotist I've ever known. That night meant nothing." Her voice had an odd, choked sound.

"Oh, but you're wrong." His low voice was as smooth and rich as velvet. "It meant a great deal to me. Admit it, Amy. You were as starved for me as I was for you."

She made a low sputtering sound that had no translation in polite English.

"I don't think I would have made it, if you hadn't been there. I really would like to see you tomorrow," he said. "Will Sam and Lorrie be there? I'd like to see—"

"Leave Lorrie alone," Amy replied icily. "I know it never mattered much to you which one of us you dated, but—"

"You know that's not true," he said quietly.

"No, I don't."

"Amy, you're the only woman I've ever loved." His low voice was intense and sincere.

"Don't!" She sounded vulnerable, lost, not her usual composed self at all. "Don't lie to me. I can't bear it. You've had lots and lots of women. And all of them were more suitable to your nature than I was. You'll never make me believe I was special."

"You still are."

"No..." The single word was a cry of pain.

"Damn it, Amy. Would you please tell me what Lorrie's got to do with us?"

A deep chasm of emotion-charged silence seemed to separate them. Some sixth sense told him Amy was terrified.

"N-nothing! Forget I said it!" she blurted out. "I didn't mean anything."

But he knew she did.

The line went dead. She had hung up on him.

Nick set the receiver down slowly. He felt far from good about their conversation. He didn't like pushing himself on people who didn't want him. Not even his own wife.

Why the hell had she been so upset when he mentioned Lorrie?

Suddenly he was furious at the unfairness of it all. Most of all he was furious at Amy. From the first, she had refused to give him or their marriage a chance.

Nick's gaze strayed to Triple's note again. In a burst of anger and frustration he wadded it up and threw it toward the trash can, but his aim was off, and it fell soundlessly onto the plush red carpet.

A cord inside of him was beginning to unravel. He couldn't live like this much longer. It was either fight for Amy or lose her forever.

If ever a man was born to fight, it was Nick Browning. Long ago he'd been hurt so deeply and so thoroughly by both his parents that it had arrested the growth of tenderness and softness in his nature, bringing into sharp focus all those other qualities he possessed—intelligence, determination, and ruthlessness.

The one thing he was good at was fighting. And this time, with Amy, he was determined to win.

Two

The hospital waiting room, with its rows of gray vinyl chairs and couches, its little Formica-topped tables, was nearly deserted. There was only a solitary rumpled figure hunched hopelessly in a darkened corner. Beside her was a briefcase she hadn't opened and a messy pile of magazines she'd skimmed and then tossed aside. She couldn't concentrate on either the words or the pictures.

Amy Browning's long black hair was lank and uncombed. Half of it was still pinned in its neat little knot; the other half streamed down her back, a mass of tangles and pins. Her young-looking face was thin and drained of color. Circles of exhaustion ringed her haunted eyes.

No one would have recognized this frightened woman as the hard-driving businesswoman she was. She'd climbed to the top by sheer force of will. When it came to money she could be as hard as nails. But when it came to her family, she was soft.

Amy's fingers were folded together tightly in her lap over her wrinkled wool skirt. Her eyes squeezed shut as she said a desperate, silent prayer.

Dear God, Please don't let my baby die!

It was February. Outside the thick walls of the hospital, a fierce storm howled down from the Gulf of Alaska and battered the city of Los Angeles and its environs. Waves tore gaping holes in the beaches and undermined the foundations of seawalls and expensive beach houses so that they tumbled into the sea. In the hills, where there had been fires the summer before, there were floods and mud slides. Gale-force winds swept across the city, shattering windows in high rises and littering the streets with shards of glass, flattening palms along the wide boulevards, blowing Mexican tiles off the roofs, crumpling highway signs and downing power lines. In the Santa Monica Mountains a blizzard raged.

It was the storm of the century, newsmen said, but Amy was scarcely aware of it.

Behind the closed doors of the intensive care unit her son, Triple, was fighting for his life.

Viral encephalitis, the doctor had said.

Amy was alone. Utterly and forlornly alone.

Dear God, where was Lorrie? Why hadn't she come as she had promised? How could anything be more important to her than Triple's life?

As always, Amy, who'd spoiled Lorrie worse than their own mother would have, had she lived, tried to rationalize her younger sister's failure to be of support when it was Amy who was in trouble. Not once in the past two days had her sister dropped by. Although Lorrie had given other excuses, Amy guessed it was because she was too involved with her acting career.

Lorrie had never been strong enough to cope with her own problems, much less with anyone else's. She was a gentle, quiet, some might think ineffectual woman. Amy was the person everyone in the family leaned on. None of them probably had any idea how close she was to a total collapse. Amy was the rock, the foundation of their lives. Amy was always in control.

A shudder swept through her slender body.

But not now. Oh, not now!

Sam Holland, Amy's father, was at home, his own health too precarious to endure the arduous wait at the hospital. While Lorrie hadn't bothered to call, Sam had phoned faithfully every hour on the first day. Later he'd stopped. It was as though he'd sensed that his calls merely added to Amy's tension. They'd emphasized the grim fact that Triple was not getting well.

Amy glanced at the sensible quartz watch she always wore. It was still an hour until visiting hours started. Then she would have only fifteen minutes with him.

She remembered how thin Triple had been when she'd seen him last. He'd been unconscious, his little face as white and bloodless as his pillowcase, so different from the vital six-year-old of two days before.

Triple had inherited Nick's lusty temperament and untamable spirit and was a constant whirlwind of precocious curiosity and adventure. He'd gotten into more scrapes than most children twice his age. She'd given up chasing him, or worrying about him when he got himself into trouble; she'd stopped attempting to answer his endless battery of questions.

He was all boy, and no matter how much she nagged, his shoelaces remained untied; the knees were always worn out of his jeans; and an assortment of skateboards, bikes, or footballs littered the driveway. In his room he kept a treasured hoard of fearsome pets in jars and clumsily made cages. Usually Triple was impish and happy, but when he squared his jaw and scowled at whomever displeased him, he could throw a tantrum that his bullheaded father would have been proud of.

In Amy's eyes, even so terribly ill, Triple was the most beautiful little boy on earth. His dark lashes lay in little curled fringes against the bright flush of his feverish cheeks. His baby-fine, golden-brown hair fell across his forehead in wispy ringlets. Although his blue eyes were closed and not twinkling with their usual mischief, no one could have helped but admire the even perfection of his features and the baby-smooth texture of his skin. He had an adorable upturned nose, a heart-shaped mouth and a square jaw, too much like his father's for comfort.

Unconscious, Triple seemed angelic. Awake, he was a diminutive human volcano.

Ignoring the tubes and monitors, Amy had touched her darling boy's forehead on that last visit, and his skin had been burning hot beneath her fingertips.

She wasn't used to worrying about him. When he was a baby she'd worried herself sick over him every time he'd gotten into trouble, until finally she'd been drained of every dram of anxiety in her soul, and she'd stopped. He was so fiercely independent he seemed able to get himself out of every jam.

Only this was different. This illness was beyond even his extraordinary powers of self-preservation.

A spasm of fear gripped her. "Triple, you have to get better," she whispered. "Grandpa and Mommy...and Aunt Lorrie need you. And who will catch bugs and guppies for your snake, Geronimo?"

Amy's body curled into a ball in the vinyl chair. Oh, how she longed to see Triple chasing around the house breaking things, letting lizards loose.

"Mrs. Browning..."

She looked up to see Dr. Alsop's elderly, seamed face and wondered vaguely how long he'd been standing there.

"I'm sorry," she whispered, startled, as she attempted to rise. "I didn't hear you come in."

"Don't get up, my dear. I just dropped by to let you know that I'll be in the record room for a while. But I'll be back to check on Triple before I go home."

Dr. Alsop was Triple's pediatrician, and he'd hardly left the hospital since Triple had been brought in.

"Is Triple..." Her voice broke.

He shook his head grimly. "There's no change. Mrs. Browning, isn't there someone who could be with you?"

"No. My sister..."

"I was thinking of Triple's father."

Amy's golden eyes came alive and flashed like giant bits of bold glitter against the chalk-white pallor of her face.

"We're separated," she managed to say in a tight voice. Involuntarily she twisted the gold band of her wedding ring until it cut into her flesh like a knife.

"I know. Still..."

She was aware of Dr. Alsop's troubled gaze studying her.

"He's the last person I'd share something like this with," she said icily. "The very last."

"Is he really so terrible?"

She dug her nails into her palms. "Some people might not think so."

"But you do?"

Her thin-lipped silence was that of a person who had a bitter distaste for the subject at hand.

"Nevertheless, he is the boy's father."

"A mere accident of birth, doctor. He doesn't deserve Triple."

"He did marry you, I remember, when Triple was a year old."

"That was no favor, I assure you." Her heart was thudding violently at that hateful memory. "Please, Dr. Alsop, I have enough to cope with just worrying about Triple."

Dr. Alsop said no more, but after he left, she felt lonelier and more miserable than before. Not that her loneliness was the doctor's fault. Nor did it have anything to do with where she was or what she was doing with her life.

Nick alone had brought her that kind of pain. She loathed him for the things he'd done in the past, but for Triple's sake she endured his occasional phone calls and gifts to his son. For her son's sake she concealed her bitter contempt and endured the one-month separation from Triple every July, when her son went to San Francisco to visit his father.

With an effort she pushed Nick from her mind, and her thoughts returned to Triple. She buried her face in her hands.

If Triple died...

Outside there was the confident tread of hard-soled shoes striding briskly down the length of the glossily waxed hall floor. The door to the waiting room opened softly, and then closed behind the man who barged inside. Amy was only vaguely aware of these sounds, but instinctively, as if even in that first abrupt moment she had sensed new danger, her spine stiffened to some semblance of its usual ramrod tightness. She glanced up, her eyes dazed and unfocused.

A tall, broad giant of a man silently stood across the room from her. Even in her shattered state Amy was aware of his commanding masculine aura.

Beneath the raincoat the man wore flame-red slacks and a white shirt open at the neck. His blond hair, brown skin, and the flamboyance of his dress struck an unpleasantly familiar note, but before she had time to realize who he was, his low, huskily pitched voice sent shock waves of dread through her body.

"Hello, Amy."

Although the raspy voice sounded different—deep and frighteningly cold—she recognized it instantly.

She sucked in her breath.

It couldn't be. Not him! Not here! Not now! Her nerves clamored as she desperately fought to deny Nicholas Browning's presence. *Let me be wrong!*

Her heart had begun to race. She felt both hot and cold at once as she glanced toward the bronzed giant in the dripping raincoat who was striding purposefully toward her.

But she wasn't wrong. It was Nick. Nick with that velvet-smooth, husky voice that could make every nerve ending in her body quiver. Nick, the brashly arrogant egotist she'd once loved so intensely she'd forgotten he was the very type of man she'd always heartily disapproved of—a man who was all show and no substance. Nick with his unruly, damp gold hair falling over his brow; Nick with his sharply chiseled features and aquiline nose, his attractively sun-bronzed skin. Nick with his large, well-muscled body and that intimidating self-confidence that gave him the dashingly reckless air of a buccaneer.

Nick, the very last person she wanted to see—especially now, when she felt so exposed, so vulnerable.

Amy lifted her chin defiantly and dared to meet his gaze. His narrowed eyes were very blue, darker than usual with some deep emotion. She felt them burning across her face.

Hastily she ran her hands through her hair and tried to compose her features into a cold, unfeeling mask.

She succeeded only in looking young and frightened.

"Nicholas." His name escaped her lips, not in greeting but on a faint note of whispered fear. Emotion rushed into her throat, swelling, pushing, choking off speech and breath.

She wanted him to leave, to go away at once. "I don't have the energy to fight you," she was able to murmur.

His lips parted and she could see the tips of his even white teeth, but the smile never reached his eyes.

"Good. Maybe we'll get along for a change."

There was nothing like his sarcasm to make Amy bristle. "Just go," she whispered.

He raised his eyebrows. "Darling, I've flown halfway across the world to get here. I'm damned if I'll leave before I find out what's going on."

Darling. Though he had no right to call her that, even mockingly, the mere word was an intimate caress that made something inside her melt. Soft words came so easily to a womanizer like Nick. Romance was his way—gentleness toward women, and insincere kindness. Those things meant so much to a plain, lonely woman not used to them, but they meant nothing to him.

She rose stiffly as he made his way across the room. The floor seemed to rock unsteadily beneath her feet.

"How is he?" Nick demanded.

She turned away from him, trying to ignore his bold masculine presence, but she was aware of him in every fiber of her body.

His hand closed around her arm like a vise and he whirled her to face him.

"Damn it, Amy. Don't shut me out. Is he dead or alive?"

He towered over her. His blue eyes blazed with an anguish and fear as terrible as her own. His volatile emotions were always so close to the surface, so overpowering.

"Alive," she whispered brokenly. "I haven't seen him for nearly three hours, and he was unconscious then."

"Have you checked with the nurses' station lately?"

She twisted her hands helplessly. "I've just been sitting here."

"You mean you haven't even—" He started to say something, then checked himself as he examined her face and saw the haunted guilt creep into her eyes. "You look exhausted," he said, his low voice kinder. "I've never seen you like this before, so close to the edge. Why aren't Lorrie or your father here?"

"Dad isn't up to the strain," Amy murmured.

"And Lorrie?"

Amy bit her bottom lip and stared at him sullenly without answering. It bothered her that Lorrie hadn't come. Perversely, it bothered her even more that Nick should miss her, too.

"I—I don't know."

His handsome face hardened. She could feel his eyes ruthlessly assessing the damage anxiety and two sleepless nights had wrought on her. She had never been the beautiful, glamorous type a man with Nick's lusty appetites and gaudy tastes naturally preferred, but usually she was at least school-teacher prim and impeccably neat.

"You don't look so hot yourself," she murmured defensively. That was a lie, of course. Nick couldn't look anything but dashingly attractive.

Ignoring her insult, he reached up and gently brushed a lock of black hair out of her eyes, securing the wayward tendril behind her ear. "Always the girl who has to prove she can tough it out alone, aren't you?" he said. His hand lingered caressingly against her cheek. "I know all about toughing it out alone."

Touching a woman came easily to a man like Nick, she thought. The warmth of his fingers stirred old, unwanted memories. Once she had believed in him. Once she had loved his touching her like that. Once she'd loved him.

"Amy, he's going to make it," Nick whispered softly.

She stared at him wordlessly until he let his hand fall away.

"Sorry," he said, chagrined by her look. "I forgot."

He looked tired, too, she thought. He was far from his flashy, suave self. His coat was rain drenched. His parrot-bright clothes were as untidy as hers. His golden hair was wet and lay matted against his dark brow.

Amy remembered vaguely the storm outside.

"I know I probably look a mess," he said, shrugging out of his raincoat and tossing it across the back of a vinyl chair over her own jacket. "I just got in from Holland. I've got a bad headache and a case of jet lag that won't quit. When Sebastian called I was with Hans at the lab going over the tank test results or our latest yacht design for Sebastian's next America's Cup campaign. I dropped everything and took a cab to the airport. My clothes are still in Amsterdam. The flight was hellishly bumpy."

"You always were a big sissy when it came to planes."

"Big sissy, hell," he growled. "It was a miracle we got down at all."

"You needn't have put yourself through all that. There wasn't any reason for you to come," she said woodenly.

For a long moment his fathomless blue eyes bored holes in her. She almost regretted what she'd said.

"Amy, I'm here for the duration, whether you want me or not. Is it so wrong for a father to be worried sick when he finds out his son is in the hospital? You didn't even bother to call me."

Because she hadn't wanted him to come.

"I'm your husband, Amy, despite the way you try to forget it. That gives me certain rights." His low, gravely tone was harsh with mockery.

He raised his hand to curve it possessively along her slender throat, exerting mastery as he turned her face toward his. "Amy..." His furious gaze held her eyes for an endless moment.

What he'd meant to do or say neither of them would ever know, because suddenly his touching her changed everything. There had always been an inexplicable physical bond between them, and even now, when she hated him, she felt its pull. The shock of it made her shudder.

Dimly she realized she should be fighting him. Instead his unexpected gentleness mesmerized her and, when she made no effort to resist him, the anger in his gaze died. All she was conscious of was the feather-light tracery of his fingers on the soft, sensitive skin of her throat. She seemed to stop breathing as his eyes explored every inch of her face.

They were both drawn, although neither wanted to be.

He had claimed that as her husband he had certain rights. Had she been rational, she would have argued that in their marriage that wasn't true. But the words wouldn't come as she felt her body being arched toward his by powerful muscular arms.

His shoulders seemed to enclose her. She felt herself being molded against the hard contours of his male length.

His fingers twined into her long black hair, and he pulled her head back. His brilliantly blue eyes burned into hers for what seemed like forever, and she felt a ripple of the old unwanted excitement.

Her throat went as dry as dust. In spite of everything, she wanted him to hold her.

She closed her eyes helplessly.

For a split second Nick's warm mouth hovered over hers, so close she could almost taste him. In another moment she would have been lost.

A rush of cold air swept into the room as the waiting room door swung open. Dr. Alsop hurried toward them, his thick fingers sifting the pages of a fat chart.

Breathing erratically, Amy sprang free of Nick's arms, stumbling backward. She felt ashamed of her reaction to him. Immediately she turned this emotion into fury toward Nick.

As for Nick, he stood statue still and regarded her with equal coldness. It never occurred to her that he might be feeling just as wary, having discovered the power she still held over him.

Amy flushed under the doctor's frankly speculative gaze. It was humiliating to have been caught in Nick's arms, especially after their earlier conversation. "It's all right, Dr. Alsop. This is Nick Browning, my...er..." She met the hot, scathing brilliance of Nick's eyes, and her faltering voice failed her.

"Her husband," Nick drawled politely, offering one hand to the older man and encircling Amy's waist with his arm, as if boldly defying her to challenge his right to do so. "I was in Holland. I wanted to get here as quickly as I could, so I had to spend most of the night on a plane."

Amy's blush deepened as Nick drew her tremulous body more closely against his own. Although she was still shaking, it maddened her that his grip was rock hard, that he seemed totally unaffected by what had nearly happened between them.

Dr. Alsop's eyes gleamed with interest. After a second or two he took Nick's hand and heartily pumped it. "I'm glad you're here. She hasn't eaten or slept since we admitted Triple. You've got two patients to worry about, young man."

"How is Triple, doctor?" Amy pleaded, desperate to change the subject.

The doctor's face masked all emotion. "We have the results of his spinal tap. He's no better, but he's no worse, either. I wish I had happier news, but I'm afraid we still have a very sick little boy on our hands. At this point, it could go either way. His condition may improve or it may deteriorate. There could be permanent brain damage, but sometimes children will recover fully within two to four weeks. If he can just hold on, he still has a chance."

"A chance..." At the thought of Triple dying, something inside Amy broke. "That's all you can promise me? A miserable chance?" She remembered the night her mother had died, and she began to sob quietly. "Doctor, if that child dies, I'll die, too."

"Mrs. Browning, we're doing everything we possibly can to save him."

But the doctors had done everything before, she thought.

"Will it be enough?" Her normally controlled voice was rising.

"Darling," Nick said gently, understanding her pain because it was his own. "Dr. Alsop wants to save Triple just as much as you do. You have to believe that." His arm tightened supportively around her, his other hand reaching up to brush her hair out of her eyes.

Nick was the last person she wanted to comfort her, especially after what had just happened between them. "Let go of me," she cried, stiffening as he pulled her even closer.

"Shhh. You're hysterical, Amy," came the low, hatefully soothing voice.

"If I'm hysterical, whose fault is that?"

His grip merely tightened.

"No," she protested.

"Amy, honey. I'm here to take care of you."

"I don't need you."

"Yes, you do. You're just too stubborn to admit it."

As she struggled to free herself, she caught glimpses of his anxious face. The skin was pale beneath his tan, but he'd set his jaw in hard, determined lines. It was in his nature to take over, to command, to subdue.

Amy twisted and bent every way against the iron grip of his arms until her frantic heart felt near to bursting. She didn't need anyone. She hadn't needed anyone in years. Not since the boating accident when she'd been a child and her mother had been drowned and her father crippled.

No, it was the other way around—everyone else needed her.

"Amy, don't fight me."

Nick's arms were a vise choking off her breath, and no matter what she did, they stayed around her. Her legs brushed against his hard thighs; his body was as tough and unyielding as steel.

It was no use. No use fighting Nick. He was too big, too powerful, too determined. At last she let herself collapse against him, panting, breathless. Her head nestled against his shirt and her scalding, bitter tears fell against his chest, spotting the white silk fabric. She could feel the warmth of him seeping into her. His hand gently stroked her mussed hair.

"Amy, he's my son, too."

She felt his great body tense with his desperate pain, and her hatred dissolved. Tenderly she reached up and brushed his rough cheek.

She relaxed in his arms, realizing how nice it was to be held, to be comforted. How drawn she was to Nick's masculine strength, how much she needed it.

Amy was aware of his palm molding itself to the curve of her throat, his long fingers sliding into the tumbled length of her hair at the back of her neck. His other hand now cupped the side of her tear-dampened face, lifting her chin with his thumb until her eyes met his.

"It's going to be all right, darling, I promise you."

A tremor of vulnerability shivered down her spine. How did he know? How could he possibly know? Yet even though believing him defied all logic, his words made those inner screaming voices of insidious doubt grow fainter.

Weakly Amy's hand fumbled for Nick's waist, and she held on to him.

Dr. Alsop said softly, "I could prescribe a sedative."

"Maybe later. Right now I want to make sure she gets something to eat." While he spoke Nick kept stroking the length of her hair, and his velvet voice and gentle touch were infinitely soothing.

"Doctor, I want to see Triple," Nick demanded.

The doctor nodded. "I'll see what I can do."

Dr. Alsop made the necessary arrangements for them to slip into the intensive care unit before visiting hours. Beneath the disapproving glare of the head nurse, whose surly expression was that of a marine drill sergeant who'd been crossed, they stared quietly at their unconscious child. Father and mother clung to one another, bound together by the terrible bond of mutual anguish. When the nurse ordered them to leave, Nick led a reluctant Amy quietly back to the waiting room, where they sat silently for a long time, holding on to each other.

As they sat together, Amy found it impossible to summon the hatred she'd felt toward Nick for years, or even her fear of him. Maybe it was only because she was so numb with terror over Triple, but she actually felt stronger because Nick was there.

Almost before Amy realized what was happening, Nick had taken command of her and of her life, precisely as he had in the past. The cynical side of her nature would have said it was just his way. He had the ruthless instincts of a predator. He always waited for the right moment—when she was most vulnerable—and then he moved in for the kill.

That was exactly the method he'd used to force her to marry him.

But at that moment she was too vulnerable and grateful for his presence to make such a cynical assessment of his character.

Revitalized, Amy felt a surge of resentment as she watched Nick wolf down two bags of chips and a ham sandwich oozing with mayonnaise.

She was reminded that he had other lusty, uncurbed appetites.

"It's positively indecent the way you enjoy your food when Triple . . ."

Nick looked up, surprised at the bitterness in her voice. "How would starving myself help Triple?" he demanded with infuriating male logic.

Silently Amy wadded up an empty potato-chip wrapper in disgust and tossed it onto her tray.

He glanced at the half-eaten, cold, cheese-on-rye sandwich in front of her. "And you'd better finish that," he ordered, "if you know what's good for you."

She felt a pang of guilt. Although Triple was no better, she herself felt much stronger. She hated Nick, but he had always made her feel vitally alive when he was around. It was as if battling him recharged some essential part of her.

Nick had taken charge—cajoled her into combing her hair, washing her face, putting on lipstick, resting and eating. He'd had Dr. Alsop call in a renowned pediatric neurologist, and new experimental medicines were being administered to their son.

Nick was staring at her from across the table, in that determined way of his. A flash of her usual stubbornness flared. She shoved the sandwich away.

He pushed it back. His fingertips grazed hers, and she flinched at the flash of heat contact with his skin brought to her body.

"Eat, darling," he insisted.

She jerked her hand away from his and stared hard at him. "Stop calling me that."

"Maybe I will—if you eat," he whispered.

She was aware of his coiled impatience, of her own fierce tension, and finally her gaze fell before the compelling force of his. She lifted her sandwich and took a tiny bite. The bread was stale and the cheese was cold and tasteless.

"I want to get back upstairs," Nick said, "but we're not going until you finish that sandwich. We've only got a little while until visiting hours start. I wouldn't want to miss seeing Triple because of your stubbornness."

"My stubbornness?" she demanded.

"Yes, of course, yours. I'm determined now because I have to be when I'm around you, that's all," he said.

"Excuse me if I don't see the difference."

"Eat, Amy." He glanced at his watch again. "If you want to see Triple, you've got five minutes."

Normally she would never have allowed him to dominate her so thoroughly, but she ate all of her sandwich—in a sullen silence that was so thick he made no attempt to interrupt it until they were back in the waiting room.

It was one minute until visiting hours.

"Triple seemed fine when I saw him at Christmas," Nick said. "You haven't told me how all this started."

"He just got sick suddenly during the night. I heard him cry out in his sleep. I went to his room, and he was burning up with fever. I rushed him to the emergency room." Her tremulous voice lowered. "I've been here ever since."

"Darling, I know it's been awful for you," he murmured.

There was that word again. It made her feel so vulnerable. Every muscle in her body stiffened.

"You said you wouldn't call me that."

His hand folded over hers, and her pulse jumped beneath his fingers. He turned her hand over in his palm and studied it thoughtfully. "I said maybe."

Through his densely curling lashes, he studied her. Amy didn't dare lift her eyes to his.

He was impossible. He always had been and always would be. But despite her fierce determination to despise him, she was reluctant to let go of the strong hand holding hers.

Why did Nick have to be the only person with whom she could share her maternal anguish?

Because he was the father of her only son.

For years she had tried to dismiss the importance of that simple biological fact. For years she had tried to convince herself that the biology of parenthood was not nearly as important as the actual parenting. For years she had tried to tell herself that Nick didn't belong in their lives, that she was capable of raising Triple alone.

Nick had told her she was wrong, but she'd refused to listen.

Now she wondered how she'd ever summon the strength to send him away again.

Her fingers tightened in his, and she held on to him.

Triple was as still and gray faced as death. There was no change, the female drill sergeant in white explained. He was holding on, but just barely.

Fresh horror gripped Amy. His eyes seemed more sunken, and beneath his white skin, his cheekbones stood out like batons in a sail.

Amy looked at all the criss-crossing tubes, Triple's IV, the oxygen mask covering his mouth and nose and the little lights blinking with bright regularity on the monitors. The room smelled faintly of antiseptic.

As Amy watched, Nick leaned over and pressed Triple's hot, limp fingers. "Triple, it's your dad. I'm here, and I'm not leaving until you're well."

Not by a flicker of an eyelash did Triple respond. Heat fairly radiated from his flushed face.

"I'm here," Nick repeated. "Can you hear me, Triple?"

Amy held her breath.

There was no sound other than the metallic rattling of the air-conditioning vent.

"He doesn't hear you, Nick," Amy said hopelessly. "Oh, I'm so afraid he'll never..."

Nick sensed how close she had come again to the breaking point. "I think we'd better go," he said.

"No. I want to stay with my baby. I have to stay with him. I..." She touched Triple's forehead. "Oh, Nick, he's burning up."

"Hush, darling," Nick murmured hoarsely. He brought his fingers gently to her lips as if to seal them. "I think the crisis will come tonight," he said. "I know it's hard for you to leave him here alone, but it's just as hard for me."

Amy looked into her husband's bleak eyes and saw a pain as terrible and profound as her own. His handsome face was haggard with anxiety. Nick needed her every bit as much as she needed him.

Without thought she slowly put her arms around him, and offered him the only thing she could, the warmth and comfort of her body. She had him in her arms, her face pressed against the roughness of his cheek. When she felt his large body shudder against hers, she just hugged him until finally he let her go.

Stiffly, blindly, like two sleepwalkers they stumbled toward the waiting room.

Later in the night, it became so cold that she began to shiver. He took care of her, wrapping her snugly first in her own light jacket and then in his oversize raincoat. He stretched out on the sofa and pulled her down beside him.

"Get some sleep, Amy," he whispered, pushing her raven head down on his lap when she made a feeble show of resistance. "Forget how you feel about me. We're in this thing together." With a weary sigh he let his own head fall back against the cushion.

Sleep. She wondered vaguely if she could ever sleep again, but she lacked the strength to argue with him.

Instead she let her cheek obediently rest upon the firm warmth of his thigh. Even though she was determined to watch him warily, it wasn't long before her eyelids started to droop. His masculine profile blurred.

She forgot the danger of him and relaxed in his arms. Soon she slept the deep, still sleep of a person utterly exhausted while behind the closed doors of the intensive care unit, their son battled for his life.

Three

———

An icy fear knotting his stomach, Nick held Amy in his arms. Throughout the long night he was afraid as he hadn't been afraid since Jack's fatal motorcycle accident two years before. Jack had fought for his life for three days and three nights, but in the end he'd lost.

Losing the brother who'd always hero-worshiped him had devastated Nick. In many ways he loved the wild and boisterous Triple exactly as he'd loved his wild and boisterous younger brother.

It couldn't happen all over again. He couldn't lose Triple the same way he'd lost Jack. He still dreamed of Jack, still missed him.

Dear God, not Triple, too! Nick knew if he lost Triple he would lose Amy as well.

He remembered his last visit with his son right before Christmas, and he was glad that he'd gone against Amy's will and seen Triple. Brief though their visit had been, Triple had been thrilled to see him.

The little boy had taken him into the garage and shown him Amy's catamaran. He had bounded onto the twin hulls with the sprightly agility of a small monkey and precociously pointed out what everything was.

"Could you teach me how to sail her, Dad? I mean *really* sail her?"

"I thought you already knew how. Sebastian sent me a picture of you and your mother."

"'Course I know how, Dad," Triple had proclaimed with his usual lack of modesty. "Only Mom doesn't think so, and she said she's not going to let me sail her anymore 'cause she says I don't do what she says on a boat. I bet if you taught me how, she'd change her mind. And I bet pretty soon I could sail so fast I could beat every kid around here. 'Specially Elgin Ferris."

"This is a mighty tough boat for a little boy to start off with," Nick had said, laughing. But he'd promised Triple that when summer came, he'd teach him how to sail. "I might have to get you your own boat."

Triple jumped down from the boat with a single, foolhardy leap. Shining blue eyes gazed eagerly up into Nick's. "My own boat, huh? Maybe I could spend the whole summer with you instead of just July."

"Maybe..."

Nick had realized then that he should have fought Amy long ago for more time with Triple. Instead, he'd buried himself in his work and sailing races and had ignored what was really important—his son.

No more, he vowed, glancing at the sterile hospital walls. Not after coming this close to losing Triple. If Triple lived, Nick was determined to change things. He was through with letting Amy call the shots. He'd let her use him to suit her own purposes long enough.

The delicate floral scent of Amy's perfume rose to Nick's nostrils. Her fingers clutched at his arms as she whimpered in her sleep from some bad dream. He glanced down at the tousled dark head in his lap and saw pain flicker across her pale features.

Even in her sleep, she was suffering. Whatever she felt toward him, she loved their son. Nick felt a rush of protectiveness toward her. He wished he could help her get through this as she'd helped him when Jack had died.

She moaned softly, burrowing her head into his belly in an intimate way that would have deeply shamed her had she been awake. Through the thin silk of his shirt he felt her hot mouth nuzzle against his flesh.

He caught his breath at a sudden flash of unwanted desire. Again her hands clutched him, as if she were seeking to bury herself in the warmth of his body.

Almost involuntarily his hand came to rest on her head. He smoothed the wispy strands of black silk into place, touching her lightly for fear of waking her. In the dim light with her inky lashes curling against her pale cheeks, her delicate features softened by sleep, she was very lovely.

Still asleep she called his name. He felt a sudden tearing pain in his whole being. More than anything he wanted Triple to live. And he wanted his wife. It didn't matter that she'd used him and married him only when he'd forced her.

Dr. Alsop led Amy and Nick into the intensive care unit. "I know it isn't visiting hours, but Triple's so much better this morning, I knew you'd want to see him. He's been awake, and his fever's down."

"Then the crisis is past?" Nick demanded.

"Maybe not entirely, but he's definitely much improved."

Dr. Alsop knocked on Triple's door and pushed it gently ajar. "I wouldn't stay too long. After what he's been through, he'll tire easily."

As they stepped inside, a single shaft of wan sunlight streamed through a high window and touched Triple's hair. It gleamed like dark gold against his pale skin. He was no longer flushed, and a slight sheen of perspiration beaded his forehead. To Amy he looked like a sleeping angel.

"Triple," she whispered.

Triple's eyes opened drowsily. He managed a thin smile for his mother, and then a bigger one for his father, which produced a gnawing ache in Amy's stomach. "Dad, I knew you'd come," he whispered. Triple clutched Amy's hand weakly when she touched his fingers. "Didn't you just know he would, Mom?" His blue eyes were big and trusting as he gazed at her.

Only for a second did the shock of her son's eager questions register on Amy's face. She was too aware of Nick's piercing gaze.

"I should have known it," she replied evasively, letting her lashes fall to veil her eyes. She felt an uneasy prick of conscience. His father's presence meant so much to Triple, and for five years she'd done everything she could to keep them apart.

"Dad, you're going to stay for a while, aren't you? You're not leaving the minute I get better, are you? Mom, you'll make him stay, won't you."

A twinge of guilt raced through Amy. "Triple, your father's a very busy man," she said softly. "We can't expect him to stay too long when he has to run South Sails with its branches all over the United States. Not to mention all of his racing commitments."

Amy would have said more, but when she felt Nick's hard blue gaze raking her, she swallowed the words.

Nick leaned over the bed and contradicted his wife in a deceptively smooth voice. "I won't be leaving, son—not even when you're better."

"Is that a promise, Dad?"

"That's a promise, son." Nick's cutting gaze slashed up to Amy's face as he spoke, daring her to protest. "From now on, I'm not going to let anything come between us."

Amy cringed at the words that spelled her doom and at the defiant challenge she read in her husband's eyes.

Triple's need for his father was natural. It was the circumstances of her marriage that made Nick's continuing presence a frightening prospect.

"Good." The faint word died on Triple's lips as he let his eyes droop shut. "You don't have to go just 'cause I'm sleeping, either, Dad," he murmured, his voice dying away again. He had forgotten his mother completely.

Nick smiled, a slow smile that transformed his rugged features into an expression of unbelievable tenderness.

This sweet look tore Amy to pieces. Once he had reserved it for her alone. She closed her eyes against the sharp ache of longing that assailed her as she remembered the bittersweet tenderness of their brief love affair. When she opened them again, she was glad Nick had his broad back turned toward her as he leaned over the bed holding Triple's hand.

"Excuse me," Amy murmured shakily. "I'll let you spend some time alone with him." She stumbled outside.

When Nick returned to the waiting room, he found Amy tucked into one desolate corner.

"Sulking?" he demanded, not in the mood to indulge her coldness toward him.

"No," she whispered raggedly, twisting the leather strap of her purse. She couldn't look up. She was too afraid he might read the aching emptiness in her eyes. "Damn you. Why did you have to come back?"

"He's my son, too," Nick said.

"We shouldn't be fighting over him."

There was the barest tensing of his expression. "That's exactly my point."

"Nick, you shouldn't have made a promise to Triple you don't intend to keep."

Eyes as calm as a blue winter sky met hers. "Don't worry, I didn't."

"You can't mean that you really intend to stay."

"For a while." At her frown, a bitter grimace chased across his mouth. He came closer, so close that he towered menacingly over her. "Would it really be so awful having your husband home, Amy?"

His gaze swept over her, and she was too conscious of every part of her body that his eyes touched.

"I don't feel like I have a husband," she replied sharply, rising to her feet, desperate to escape.

"Then I've definitely stayed away too long." He spoke with a deadly softness that should have warned her. "I realized that last night when I held you in my arms and almost kissed you."

Disdain glittered coldly in her eyes. "No," she murmured with tight finality. "The best thing for all of us would be for you to go away and stay out of our lives completely."

"I don't believe that anymore. Last night you needed me. When I got here you were falling apart."

"Last night I would have been fine, if you hadn't come."

"Oh, you would have?" She was edging toward the door. With the swift, savage grace of a jungle cat, he seized her by the wrist and yanked her against his body. "You lying little cheat," he muttered bitterly. "You can't even say, 'thank you, Nick, for being there when I needed you.' No, you just use me and then kick me in the gut when you're through with me." His harsh grip dug into her skin. "I'm tired of that treatment, honey."

"Nick, don't..."

"I flew across an ocean and this entire country to get back to you, to help you, but you don't want me. All you've ever wanted is my money. Or Sebastian's, once you'd used me to get ahold of him."

Words of denial sprang to Amy's lips, but she bit them back.

He pressed her against himself until every hard muscle and bone of his body imprinted themselves on her soft curves. He was burning hot, his arms crushing steel bands. "Maybe it's time you learned what marriage really means."

Her heart raced in frantic alarm. "Nick, I don't want you," she whispered breathlessly.

His hands wound into her hair. She felt his fingers digging into her scalp as he pulled her head back. She despised him, but the hard pressure of his male body against her ignited her senses. The warmth of his breath gently wafted over her lips, and his musky scent tantalized her. Every nerve in her body was treacherously aware of him.

She pushed at his arms, struggling to break their hold.

"But I want you," he said softly. His eyes were as hard as diamonds. "And maybe I'm tired of wanting and never having. You're my wife. Maybe it's time I took what I want."

Brutally he covered her lips with his, and his rough, unshaven cheek burned against her own. He kissed her hard and insolently, not caring that he hurt her, that he humiliated her.

"You are mine," he muttered hoarsely, determined to dominate her with the emotion that dominated him. "Mine."

The fierce words branded her soul. Overpowered by his masculine strength, she didn't even try to fight him. His mouth smothered hers, and blackness whirled in a mist of stars behind her closed eyelids.

She felt faint, helpless in his arms, caught in the blaze of his passion. Only when she stopped fighting him did the furious quest for revenge cease to rule him, a gentler emotion stealing into his heart. His hold didn't slacken, but instead of hurt, his mouth exerted mastery.

Intuitively sensing this change in him, her body melted into his, and slowly some emotion, long buried in the cold tomb of her heart, flared hotly alive as his lips and tongue and hands caressed her. Against her earlobe he murmured soft, heated endearments, and she could not hold back a tiny moan of surrender. She returned his kisses, softly at first, her mouth playing sweetly beneath his, and then more feverishly.

In the white heat of passion all their differences ebbed away.

"You are mine," he whispered, and she could not deny it.

When he let her go at last, she was so thoroughly shaken she would have fallen clumsily, had he not reached out and caught her gently in his arms. Only when she had regained her balance, did he let her go.

Not a word passed between them as she turned her back on him and went to the small window that looked out on the hospital parking lot.

She heard his footsteps approaching behind her, and the tiny hairs on the back of her neck prickled in awareness of him. She didn't dare to look at him, but a fierce tremor of longing shivered down her spine.

With one kiss he'd shown her that all their years apart, all her stubborn determination to hate him were as nothing against the terrible power he held over her. She had loved him, and once he had almost destroyed not only her life but the lives of the people she loved more than anything.

"Why don't you just go?" she said in a low strangled tone. "Please..."

She was aware of his hands brushing over her hair, and she quickly sidestepped to avoid his touch. But not before her heart had betrayed her and begun to flutter wildly.

He flicked the miniblinds apart. "Storm's over," he said. His voice was distant, yet warmly ironic.

She glanced indifferently at the gray, wet world revealed through the parted blinds. All she could think of was his immense body, so burningly near her own. All she could feel was an insane urge to throw herself into his arms and let him hold her once more. No matter what he'd done in the past, he had a power over her senses no other man had ever had.

"I think it's time I drove you home," he began, "so we can both shower and change and get some rest."

His matter-of-fact suggestion created a chaos of emotion. He was closing in on her, taking over, ordering her around as if it were his right to do so.

One kiss, and he thought he owned her.

Amy whirled around.

For a numbed moment, she could only stare mutely at him.

In the gray light his blue eyes flashed with the glint of icy steel as he regarded her down the arrogant length of his aquiline nose. She noted the commanding thrust of his jaw—never a good sign—the startling prominence of his chiseled cheekbones and the cynical lines slashed on either side of his hard mouth. His was always an uncompromisingly masculine face, but at the moment, he looked so

ruthlessly determined she knew that only a fool would dare
to stand up to him.

Her own jaw squared. "No. I don't want to go home with
you," she said stubbornly.

"Look," he said, "I'm too tired to argue."

Amy felt a mild pang of unwanted sympathy for him. It
wasn't only exhaustion that had etched those lines beneath
his eyes and beside his lips.

"I can't leave Triple," she insisted. "I have to be here
when he wakes up again."

"If you don't look after yourself, you're not going to be
much use to Triple when he does get better. I've already left
your telephone number at the nurse's station in case there's
an emergency while we're gone."

"Nick!"

"There's no use arguing." He snapped the miniblinds
shut. His hand wrapped around her elbow, his fingers biting into her flesh as he propelled her across the room to the
chair where they'd left their things. He picked up her jacket
and purse and shoved them into her reluctant arms.

"You always win, don't you?" she murmured angrily as
he pulled on his raincoat and then helped her into her jacket.

She felt his touch graze the nape of her neck as he pressed
the collar of her jacket flat. Abruptly her body stiffened.

A dark flush colored his cheeks. "With you it's never
easy."

"Sunday driver!" Nick muttered fiercely, jamming his
right heel down hard on the accelerator.

Amy's heart lurched as the tires screamed around a curve
and the car shot forward on a fresh burst of speed. She
clutched the handles of her briefcase so tightly her fingers
ached as Nick caught up to a pickup and zoomed past it.

"Pretty sunset," Nick said mildly, impervious to her fear as he glanced over his left shoulder at the scarlet dazzle that splashed ocean and sky. At the same time he noted the pickup in his rearview mirror with male satisfaction.

"If you're going to drive like a maniac, you could at least keep your eyes on the road," Amy sputtered nervously. Up to this point, they had driven in tense silence ever since he'd roared out of the hospital parking lot twenty minutes ago.

A faint smile played at the edges of his mouth, and for a minute she thought he was going to make a sarcastic retort. To her surprise, Nick lazily turned his attention back to the road. His gaze slid to her, brief and sweeping. "Whatever you say, sweetheart."

Her mouth was tautly compressed, her nerves even more gratingly on edge than before.

The daylight was fading. Mud slides had carved new fissures in the Santa Monica Mountains, and several homes dangled precariously from the edge of a cliff. In places the road was blocked. Over the Pacific the sky was very high, rinsed by the storm's deluge to a pale, clear lavender. Little tufts of cloud drifted on a wet, cold wind, nestling into the pockets between the hills. A red sun hung low against the horizon, gilding the ocean's placid surface with streamers of blood-red fire.

All Amy saw was the wet asphalt whipping beneath the blue hood of her Oldsmobile, and it was too much for her. "You're not racing a twelve-meter in the Indian Ocean, you know," she said tightly.

"I know." After a deliberate pause he continued. "But, honey, I've got a hell of a lot more at stake in this contest."

He braked slightly, probably only because her driveway was in sight. Tires spun gravel as he skidded to a stop a fraction of an inch from her Wedgwood-blue garage door.

"Home at last," he murmured. A corner of his mouth lifted cynically as he eyed the charming redwood establishment nestled against a low dune.

Home. Never before had the word struck such an ominous note of doom in her heart. Just for a second her eyes darted toward him.

His chiseled profile was backlighted by golden-red light, its lines as hard and unyielding as those of a tyrannical emperor stamped on some ancient coin. Nick looked indomitable.

He was her husband. She found this fact distinctly chilling.

"Yes," she agreed. "Home. At last. I never thought I'd reach it alive."

Low, harsh laughter came from his throat. "Oh, you're very much alive." His hand reached across the distance between them and traced the soft flesh of her upper arm before she jerked it furiously away. His voice became low and sexy. "Believe me, honey, that's exactly how I want you."

She wasn't ready for the sudden softening of his tone, like a caress of velvet sliding against sensitive skin. "I thought I made it clear I didn't want you touching me," she said.

"Honey, that may be the message you thought you meant to send," came his treacherously raspy voice, "but it's not the message I got." With sickening accuracy, he continued, "You wanted a lot more than I could give you in a hospital waiting room. Maybe now that we're home..."

"Not if I can help it!" she whispered.

His eyes bored into hers. "But you can't," he said.

He let his veiled gaze glide over her face and figure in silent admiration, and he grinned broadly as if he were contemplating some delightful prospect.

"You don't know what you're talking about!"

"Wait and see." The smug half smile lingered on his lips.

Scorching waves of shame splashed her cheeks with spots of fire. She longed to think of some stinging retort that would set him properly in his place.

Instead she snatched her keys from the ignition and threw open her door. Then she sprang out of her car and rushed up the brick path to her front door. The hushed sound of his laughter followed her. Then his car door slammed.

She was sifting through her purse for her house key, when his hand closed around her wrist.

"I'll find it," he said.

A shiver of apprehension raced icily over her flesh at his touch. Swiftly he located the key. As he was pulling it out, she tried to jump away, but he caught her by the shoulders and held her against his body.

"We wouldn't want anyone to think I wasn't welcome in my own home," he murmured silkily.

"Why not, if it's the truth?"

He said nothing, but there was the barest tightening of Nick's square jaw as he inserted the key in the door. Before he could unlock it, the lock rattled from the inside, and the door was suddenly thrown open by a dark middle-aged woman, with a thick coil of iron-gray hair perched precariously on top of her head. A pair of grubby gardening gloves protruded from the pockets of the woman's worn apron.

At first Apolonia registered shock at the sight of her embarrassed mistress in the arms of her estranged husband. Then her stoic Indian face burst into the radiant smile that was normally reserved solely for Triple.

"Mr. Neecholas," she cried with uncustomary exuberance, her black eyes growing brilliant as she ignored her mistress's scowl and concentrated on the golden giant looming in the doorway. "I'm so glad you here!"

Nick released Amy and swept the short woman into his arms, giving her a hearty bear hug that lifted her off her feet. "Of course, I'm here," he said, gently mocking Apolonia's accent. "The prodigal husband has come home—where he belongs."

"Mr. Neek, we missed you so much. I go to the kitchen now, and make you something good to eat."

Although he seemed to be smiling down at Apolonia broadly, he was watching Amy too. "Now, that's the way to welcome a man home."

Amy paled at the sharp thrust of Nick's double-edged barb. Did he never miss an opportunity to bait her?

"I been using the gloves you give me for Christmas," Apolonia said proudly, patting the pocket at her thick waist as he set her down once more.

"So I see. But I hope you've been rattling those pots and pans in the kitchen."

Apolonia never liked thinking about cooking and cleaning, the job she'd been hired to do. "How is Triple, Mr. Nick," she said quickly, craftily changing the subject to the little boy they both loved.

"He's better."

"Mr. Nick, Mr. Sebastian, he send some clothes over for you."

"Great."

"I put them in Triple's room."

"Apolonia, I do believe you've lost weight."

"I been sick with the flu, but I feel better now. And, Mr. Nick, Mr. Sebastian, he wants you to call him about business...."

Amy sneaked past the effusive pair and left them babbling in the doorway as she moved on into her house, down the long hall toward her bedroom, grateful for once that the cement-headed Apolonia, who had rarely shown more than the mildest feelings of warmth toward the woman who had faithfully employed her for nearly five years, adored Nick.

Amy was about to open her door, when she heard her father's voice behind her.

Turning, she saw a frail, hump-shouldered figure step from the den into the dim hallway. Behind him rose the blare of the television.

"Is that Nick I hear?" Sam asked, his eager voice suddenly choked with emotion.

"Who else would Apolonia abandon her potted plants for and offer to cook a meal for?"

Sam smiled. "Triple must be better or you two wouldn't be here."

Amy nodded. "He's conscious now, and his fever's down."

"Honey, why didn't you tell me Nick was coming?" Her father gave her a searching look.

"Because I was hoping he would leave as soon as Triple was out of danger," she snapped truthfully.

"Sam!" Nick's voice boomed down the hall. The next second he had joined them. "I can't tell you how great it is to see you!"

Nick's white grin transformed his dark face, and just for a second Amy felt herself softening. Then her blood turned to ice as she realized how susceptible she still was to Nick's false brand of charm. If she didn't know better, she might almost have believed he cared something for Sam.

"Amy, you can go now. I'll see to Sam." Nick waved her away, dismissing her imperiously as if she were of no importance.

She had longed to escape him—until he told her to.

"Well?" Nick drawled offensively, one of his eyebrows arching in her direction when she remained.

"I'll stay, thank you," she grumbled perversely.

"Suit yourself," came his indifferent reply. He turned back to her father.

Sam's smile was almost as silly and warm as Apolonia's had been as Nick shook his father-in-law's hand affectionately. Sam's faded eyes were shining with blissful happiness, and it upset Amy to see her own father thirstily drinking in the sight of the one man who'd shattered all their lives.

Nick ignored her coldness and switched on the lights in the den. The relaxing, cozy room was decorated with African masks and furnished with Mexican rawhide chairs. A rumpled blue blanket at the foot of the couch and an untidy stack of newspapers on the floor told of Sam's lonely vigil while Amy had been at the hospital.

"This place is as dark as a tomb. I bet you haven't eaten a home-cooked meal in days," Nick said.

The answer was all too apparent, and the brief accusing glance Nick gave Amy made her squirm with guilt.

She met his gaze with a withering scowl that would have daunted a less forceful man.

"Well, now that I'm here, all that is going to change. Sam, you've endured Apolonia's bullying too long. And Amy's, too."

"Mine?" Amy shot Nick a dark look, but he just grinned boldly back at her, pretending he didn't see her anger as he marched across the den. He stopped in the middle of the room, eyeing a scarred chessboard tucked beneath a pile of magazines. He went over to the board and picked it up, studying it thoughtfully.

"Do you still play chess, Sam?"

"Not since you left." The wealth of loneliness in his reply pulled at Amy's heart. Never once had she offered to play with him.

"Me neither," Nick said with grave sincerity as he set the board down. "But that's something I'm going to change, too."

Amy drew in a deep, furious breath. Enough was enough! Watching Nick take command of her disloyal household was unendurable. "You won't be here long enough to change anything."

Nick's eyes met hers, and he smiled, though not as cordially as before. He yanked the proper cords, and the drapes danced open. "I wouldn't count on that, darling, if I were you." His voice was very quiet, but it filled the room, grating, like rough stones grinding together.

The sun had sunk below the horizon, but rich burgundy streaks painted the sky and ocean. The surf was high. The beach was littered with driftwood and other bits of broken flotsam, mute evidence of the waves that had ravaged it only hours before.

"I always forget how beautiful the view is here," Nick was saying, speaking more to himself than to them.

He could never resist the water. He opened a glass door and stepped outside into the briskly cold, salt-scented air.

He was glad to get out of the house, away from Amy. Her hostility bothered him more than he had any intention of showing her.

A gull screamed and dived toward the sparkling waves. It flapped away, something caught in its beak.

Nick shut the door and drew a deep breath to ease his tension. He felt like a knight that had just breached the walls of his enemy's castle. It didn't matter that he was exhausted from the battle. He'd fought his way inside, and he intended to stay—for as long as it took him to get what he wanted.

Nick's eyes scanned the magnificent house that spilled over its hill. The redwood beach house was mansion-size, modern and bold in design with skylights, trestled ceilings and immense windows that looked out on the ocean. He'd bought it to make Amy happy. She'd hated it and Malibu on sight.

At the bottom of the hill a vine-covered pergola curved around an immense, glassed-in swimming pool. The surrounding gardens, Apolonia's favorite domain, were perfectly groomed. There were jacaranda trees and Lebanese cedars, ivy-clad stone walls, beds of purple and red flowers, their petals battered and limp from the storm.

Nick's fingers clenched around the lightly gold-stained railing as he stared beyond the immediate grounds to the flat, rapidly darkening ocean. Amy had certainly come up in the world. Six and a half years ago she'd been a lifeguard at the yacht club, working her way through UCLA. She'd been poor but smart and awesomely ambitious. Then she'd met Nick and through him, his father's cousin Sebastian. She'd used her pregnancy to worm her way into Sebastian's heart, and more importantly his wallet. It baffled Nick that Sebastian trusted her so implicitly and wouldn't listen to a word of criticism concerning her.

Working for Sebastian, Amy had gone straight to the top. For all her softness toward her family, she could be hard when it came to business, to money. Now she lived in a colony of movie stars and wealthy international celebrities.

What a fool he'd been not to realize what she'd been after. All he'd seen was her softness, her innocence. He'd even admired her determination and ambition.

He wondered if the money and success had made Amy happy. Was she ever lonely? Did she ever ache for a man with whom to share her life as he ached for a woman? Or were her governing emotions only greed and ambition?

No matter what happened, no matter how she fought him, he wasn't leaving until he had the answers.

Four

The hot water ran through Amy's freshly lathered hair and soaked into her skin. Whorls of steam twined around her. Amy felt she could have stood forever in that tiled compartment with the sweet-scented warmth flowing over her body. If only Nick hadn't invaded her territory and upset the equilibrium of her life.

Closing her eyes, she turned her face into the nozzle and tried to forget him as shampoo bubbles rushed down the curve of her back, pooling in a soft mountain of foam at her toes.

But she couldn't forget him. Memories from the past swirled in her mind like the mists swirling around her body.

Amy had been a young and vulnerable twenty when Nick burst into her life like a tornado. She and Lorrie had had summer jobs at the Riviera Yacht Club at Newport Beach where Nick was a member. At first he was aloof, apparently too far above them to notice them.

But Amy had noticed him. Although she was proud and ambitious herself, she'd never seen anyone so brash and self-confident, so filled with purpose. She'd been instantly prejudiced against him because he was rich and handsome and because he was the cocky type all the women chased. Nevertheless, she'd watched him with an avid interest, even before he'd asked Lorrie out.

Nick had wanted to be the best sailor in the world. He wanted to win the America's Cup someday. He was nearly finished with his engineering degree, and he planned to be a great sail maker and work for his older cousin, Sebastian. At first she thought he was only bragging, but then she saw him throw himself into his sailing with an all-consuming, formidable energy as a member of the handpicked crew fine-tuning Sebastian's latest America's Cup challenger.

Amy could not help envying Nick that summer. Imagine being the son of one of the richest rancher-oilmen in the nation, even a bastard son who hadn't always felt loved and wanted as a child. Imagine being the cousin of a multimillionaire like Sebastian Jacobs, a man who thought nothing of sponsoring an America's Cup campaign.

Nick's world seemed glamorous, while hers was hard. He could have anything he wanted. Amy had had to work for everything she had. He never noticed her, but she felt curiously restless and excited whenever he was around. She found him dangerously fascinating, and she resented him because of it.

With her own mother dead, Amy had always felt responsible for her younger sister and crippled father. She felt she had to move up in the world so that she could take care of them, but it was a struggle to work, nurture her family and study.

It was one thing to observe Nick from afar; quite another when he started dating her younger, impressionable sister. After her second date with him, Lorrie had come home starry-eyed, and Amy had panicked, thinking Nick much too sophisticated and worldly for her baby sister.

The next afternoon Amy went down to his boat at the club. It had been a sparkling summer day. He was in the cabin, busy at some task, and she had interrupted him.

He'd come up through the hatch and stepped onto the deck of his gleaming white yacht, a braided coil of line dangling from his brown hand. He was shirtless and perspiring, a bronzed god of rippling golden-brown muscle. When he saw her, his expression became impatient, arrogant. Never had he seemed richer or more spoiled. Amy felt all the resentment she'd harbored against him flare up.

"Miss ... er ... ?"

It galled her that he had forgotten her name.

"Amy Holland. Lorrie's sister."

"Oh, yes. The lifeguard. I remember."

"I know you must be busy, and I shouldn't be bothering you ..." She paused, but he didn't deny her words. "It's because of Lorrie that I'm here."

"Really?" He raised his eyebrows. Brilliant blue eyes surveyed her. She had not been sure what they expressed. Disbelief—a certain cynical amusement perhaps.

Amy felt uneasy being alone with him, furious, and yet exhilarated. "Let me explain."

"Please do."

"She's only sixteen and you're twenty-two. She's a child. You're so much more sophisticated. You've had so many women. One more or less can't mean anything to you. You could date someone else. Someone older and less impressionable."

He dropped the coil of line on the deck with a thud and stepped closer, concentrating his full attention on her.

"You've obviously made quite a study of me. I hadn't re-alized I'd made such an impression."

"Y-you haven't."

"So you think I've had a lot of women?" There was a new note in his voice. A dangerous note. "So many that losing one could make no difference."

Amy felt numb with dismay. All she had done was make a fool of herself.

"Who told you that?" he asked.

"No one. I could just tell."

Again he raised his eyebrows. "So Lorrie's only six-teen?" Amy nodded. "She lied to me about that."

Amy believed him. Lorrie never lied about important things, but on rare occasions she had been guilty of telling little white lies when she wanted something badly enough.

He was watching Amy. "And you're the big sister?"

She nodded again. "By four years."

"Then you're older...and less...impressionable." Slowly, casually he inspected her in the insolent way she'd seen him admire other more beautiful women. He laughed and said, "It looks like I picked the wrong sister."

The way he looked at her made Amy feel funny inside. His casual attitude unnerved her. She was horrified by the way he'd twisted everything around. She was sure he was secretly laughing at her.

"I didn't come down here to flirt with you," she snapped.

He merely stepped closer and laughed again. She felt her cheeks blazing. He smiled down at her, as though he were very pleased about the way things were turning out.

"I'm not flirting, either," he said huskily.

She felt on fire with anger and with some new, inexplic-able emotion. "I'm just a joke to you."

"No." There was a baffling intensity in his gaze.

Amy was near tears. Before he could say more, she turned and ran down the dock, but when she looked back, she found that he was watching her still, with the same darkly intense expression in his eyes.

Why had she gone to speak to him? He'd seen through her, seen her own secret desire for him that she hadn't even seen herself. All she'd done was make a fool of herself.

He didn't call Lorrie again, and the next week, he started asking Amy out. At first she'd refused, but he'd been very persuasive. There was an immediate affinity between them. They were both ambitious and driven to excel. They loved the water and boats. All too soon they came to love each other. Even trivial occurrences seemed to take on a special importance when she shared them with him. Nick spent every free evening at her house with her, not seeming to mind the shabbiness of her family's little home. It wasn't long before their romance blossomed into a love affair. Mutual friends began to warn Amy that she was getting in too deep, that although Nick had dated many women, he had never really been serious about any of them.

At first Lorrie hadn't seemed to be bothered about Nick's asking Amy out, but as Amy fell more and more deeply in love, Lorrie's attitude began to change. At first she was only quiet when he visited. Then one night after she stumbled upon Nick and Amy kissing, the change in her became more dramatic. She seemed to go wild and started dating Nick's younger brother, Jack. He would pick her up on his motorcycle, and she wouldn't come home for hours.

When Amy expressed her concern about Lorrie dating Jack, Nick had laughed, saying that, yes, his brother could be wild at times, but Jack really liked Lorrie. Nick had told Amy he understood her urge to constantly meddle in a younger sibling's life—he was guilty of it himself sometimes—but it was an impulse one should fight.

"But Lorrie doesn't have a mother," Amy said.

"She has you, and you care for her and spoil her more than any mother would," Nick had replied. "Lorrie's lucky. If I'd ever had someone like you to love me, I wouldn't have wanted anything else." His eyes on her had softened like his words.

Amy had forgotten her initial impression of Nick and had believed he loved her—until that last night of the summer before he was to leave L.A. for Berkeley. He had taken her out for dinner, then afterward they went out on Sebastian's boat and ended up making love on it. Nick had driven Amy home, dropping her off and saying he'd return to the apartment he and Jack shared so he could pack.

Amy had promised Nick she would transfer to Berkeley and would join him in a few weeks. That night on a sudden impulse, after he'd gone she'd driven to his apartment, just to see him one last time.

Amy bit into her bottom lip as she remembered.

When she'd gotten to his apartment, she'd heard hushed voices coming from beyond Nick's door. Nick hadn't been alone. Lorrie was there too, and as Amy stood outside the door and listened, she'd heard soft cries. Every warm emotion in her heart had turned to ice.

Finally, hoping she might have made a mistake, Amy had gone to the window and peeked inside through the half-drawn shades. There was no mistaking what she saw.

Lorrie was in Nick's arms, on his bed. She wasn't wearing much. Nick was speaking to her softly. Jack was nowhere in sight.

The scene had been too incriminating for any explanation to wipe it clean. Amy had rushed home, too hurt to confront them, but somehow, Lorrie must have seen her. Later her sister had come to her and confirmed Amy's worst suspicions. She'd begged her forgiveness.

Amy remembered Lorrie's stricken, bewildered face. "I didn't mean for it to happen! I didn't! I tried to stop loving him when you started going with him, Amy. I could see how much he meant to you. I even dated Jack—to forget Nick. But he was unforgettable."

Sweet Lorrie, always trying to help and never quite managing it. "I know," Amy whispered.

"I had to see him before he left," Lorrie had continued. "I didn't mean for anything to happen, but when he kissed me, I couldn't seem to stop him."

At this point she broke into a torrent of fresh tears, and Amy's heart twisted with the agony of her hopeless love.

"It was awful. I feel so guilty. I hate him now for what he did to me. For what he did to you. And I hate myself. He never loved...either one of us. Oh, Amy, I'm so sorry. Please say it won't matter. Please say you still love me. I don't care about him. Not after..."

Lorrie's luminous eyes were wide with horror. Amy's imagination had filled with lurid images of Nick with Lorrie.

"It wasn't what I thought it'd be," Lorrie moaned darkly. "I'll never care about him again, if only you'll love me. If you stop loving me, I swear I'll die."

For all her outward glamour and beauty, Lorrie was still a child. But she was more fragile, more easily wounded than any child, perhaps because she'd lost her mother so young, and Amy had always been fiercely protective of her.

"Of course, I love you," Amy said in spite of her own pain, stroking her hair. "I'll never stop loving you."

"You can have him. I'll never go near Nick again."

"I don't want him."

Lorrie looked up. "Then Nick won't come between us."

"Never again."

"And you won't go away with him?"

Amy could feel her sister shaking.

"No."

Slowly Lorrie had quieted down.

As time passed, although Amy felt destroyed, she had tried not to blame Lorrie. Only Nick. Sometimes Amy had wanted to kill him, not just for his betrayal of her, but for what he'd done to a mere child. Lorrie was never the same after that night. Her innocence was gone, and there was always a sadness in her eyes. She rarely dated. She became more dependent than ever on Amy.

Amy saw it all so clearly. On that first day when she'd gone to speak to Nick she had broken them up, and by doing so, she had inadvertently stolen the man Lorrie had believed she loved. Lorrie had been too immature to handle this loss. Nick had decided Lorrie was too young for him and had dated her older sister instead. But his initial attraction for the more beautiful Lorrie had lingered. When she'd come to him on that last night, even after a night of lovemaking with Amy, he hadn't been strong enough to resist the temptation. He was a man of lusty appetites—a man easily aroused, and once aroused, he could be very determined. No doubt he had even regretted what had happened. But it was too late for his regrets to make any difference. For all his appeal, he'd proven he was a man of weak character, and Amy despised him.

Maybe she could have forgotten him and that awful night if only there hadn't been the baby. But then she'd been trapped after its birth. Nick had found out about Triple and had forced her to marry him.

At least Amy couldn't be sorry about Triple, no matter how much pain his birth had brought her. She loved him too dearly.

Nick was the problem, she thought, still standing in the shower. He had to go before he started making trouble all over again.

Amy turned off the water and got out, quickly toweling herself off with a thick Turkish towel and dressing in a pair of purple slacks and a voluminous pullover sweater. She dried her gleaming hair, wound it into a knot at the nape of her neck, and put on fresh makeup. While she went about these ordinary, habitual tasks, she kept wondering about Nick.

What did he intend? It was alarming the way he knew just what to say and what to do to win the loyalty of everyone close to her. Sam and Triple had always adored him, and although at first the gloomy Apolonia had presented a challenge, Nick had hastily surmounted it by pretending an interest in her gardening. As for Lorrie, Amy couldn't bear to think about their relationship. She was relieved that her sister wasn't home.

Amy had locked both her bedroom and her bathroom doors, but she'd half expected Nick to force his way inside while she was showering.

Since he hadn't come looking for her, Amy decided to go looking for him. When no one answered her soft knocks at Triple's door, she pushed it open. In the dim light she saw a suitcase spread open across Triple's bed. Masculine toilet articles littered the navy bedcovers, along with the red slacks and silk shirt Nick had been wearing.

One step into the room, and she realized she should have waited for Nick to look for her. The bathroom door opened, bounced against the door stopper, and Nick stepped boldly into the bedroom. Though she was standing in the shadows, the dazzling white light from the bathroom played over his immense body, and she had no trouble seeing him.

He was naked. For an endless moment she could only gape in breathless surprise. She felt her cheeks grow hot, and her heart begin to hammer as she struggled to focus her attention on something besides bronzed skin and well-defined muscles. But no matter how she fought it, his virile maleness held her gaze like a magnet.

He had just showered and a sheen of dampness glistened in his golden hair. The tangy scent of masculine after-shave lotion emanated from his smooth jawline. She caught the pleasant smell of fresh soap.

Black slacks and a long-sleeved blue dress shirt lay carelessly over one muscular arm. He held a towel in his other hand. She hastily averted her gaze, but not before memorizing every detail of that flawless male body, from the golden-furred planes of his hard chest to the rippling muscles of his shoulders, torso and legs. A surging ache rose from deep inside her as she longed to be held in his arms and to let her fingers glide over the moist warmth of his flushed skin.

Treacherous thought! Dear Lord! But it had been so long—two years—since she'd known anything other than the agonizing loneliness of living like a single woman—two years since she'd experienced the thrilling fulfillment only Nick could give her.

And she'd told herself that that night after Jack's service had meant nothing to her and that she wanted Nick out of her life forever!

She gasped, acutely conscious of the implied intimacy of finding Nick naked in a bedroom, even their son's.

Nick heard the sound. Amused blue eyes discovered her in the darkness and studied her mercilessly.

Amy wanted to die. Or at least to run.

She remained frozen where she was.

His throaty chuckle sent a tremor down her spine. "Well, well. Things seem to be going even better than I planned. I never expected you to come to me. And so soon."

Amy let out a low growl of fury. "I should have known you'd take this in the worst possible way."

"Or the best. Our viewpoints differ, as usual." He grinned that white-toothed, loathsome grin that could have such a devastating effect on her nerves. "Tell me, what is it you need from me? I'm always happy to be of service—to such a beautiful lady, who just happens to be my wife." He tossed his towel on the bed. His mocking tone, combined with his utter nakedness and perverse lack of modesty, gave his seemingly innocent remark an unpleasant double meaning.

Her face turned as red as a wine grape. "I don't need anything from you," she snapped. "I'll be in the living room, thank you."

"You'll stay right here," he commanded, taking a menacing step toward her.

"Not when you don't have a stitch on."

"That situation can easily be remedied," he said softly, "if you really want it to be."

She regarded him with cool silence. "You're crazy if you think I'm going to stand here and watch you dress."

Amused blue eyes sparkled. "So you prefer me nude? I had hoped so."

She emitted a muted cry. "Damn you. Stop twisting everything I say."

"Okay, okay. Look, if I don't mind dressing in front of you, why should you mind watching? It's not as if you haven't seen it all before."

"That's hardly something I want to be reminded of."

"Really?" An eyebrow arched and met the wayward lock of gold that tumbled over his brow. He looked boyish and mischievous, and so dangerously attractive that she blushed again. "Then why did you come in here?"

She was backing toward the door. "I knocked, you . . . you . . ." She searched for the worst insult in her repertoire, only to find them all hopelessly inadequate.

"Why don't you save that particular compliment for later?" he asked in a velvety, hypnotic tone.

"Compliment?" she shrieked. She had almost reached the door to the hall. "I was about to call you a bastard!"

"In my case that's only the truth. Remember?" he teased, not in the least perturbed.

She had one foot out the door.

"If you go, I'll only come after you," he taunted softly.

"Without any clothes?"

"I swear, I will."

She hesitated, recalling how he liked nothing better than to back up his obnoxious promises.

"You may remember that I love running around the house nude," he added, "especially if I'm chasing you."

"For your information I've struggled to forget everything about your odious personal habits just as I've tried to forget everything about our short-lived marriage."

He moved closer.

"Why do you keep strutting around naked?" she cried. "Why don't you get dressed?"

Without bothering to search for his underwear, he pulled on the black slacks. They hugged his male shape as tightly as a glove. She watched his bronzed hand tug the zipper up.

"I'm flattered it's been such a struggle—to forget me," he said, letting his gaze linger on her face.

Her own gaze was resting hungrily on the tanned expanse of that gold-furred chest. "You are so arrogant. You're flattered even when I insult you!"

He laughed boldly. "You could do worse, you know, than to have a man who thrives on your insults—since you love to dish them out." Then he said huskily, "Some men are not so easily pleased. You're lucky I have such a sweet disposition."

Sweet! That was the last adjective she would have applied to him. "Just get dressed," she muttered.

Feeling trapped, Amy turned her back on him and studied Triple's gruesome collection of pets while Nick took what seemed an interminable time to dress. In one jar was a tarantula. Normally its hairy legs in motion would have evoked a mild shiver of horror in Amy at the very least, but she was too wary of the dangerous man behind her. In another jar there was an immense chrysalis, which Triple inspected first thing every morning when he jumped out of bed. There were frogs, beetles, turtles and other spiders.

From behind her came the taunt of Nick's raspy voice. "It's safe to look now."

"I prefer not to." Her eyes remained glued on the hairy black legs of Triple's tarantula. Perhaps if she ignored him, Nick would leave her alone.

Nick lifted a jar of scrambling spiders. "Our Triple's certainly all boy," he said, refusing to be ignored.

Our. Why did the word make Amy tremble and want to slink away?

"Like his father," Nick murmured, his low voice a silken caress. He moved nearer. She caught his clean male scent. His voice grew even softer. "You weren't always made of ice. Don't you ever get lonely, Amy?"

"No!" She spoke sharply, breathlessly. She didn't dare to turn around.

"I do." His tone was oddly warm and gentle.

Her heartbeats sped crazily. "I'm sure there are many women..." She broke off, finding the thought surprisingly painful.

"There are, but I'm not interested."

"Maybe you should develop new interests."

Her sideways glance sought his carved profile in the dim light. His mouth was set in grim lines.

"Believe me, I've told myself that more than once, but I'm not ready to give up on you and me."

"Nick, please, I don't want to talk about us."

"You never do." He spoke quietly, but with a biting cynicism. "Amy, all my life people have shut me out. First my mother did, because I was the bastard that ruined her life. When I was a kid I knew something was wrong with me, but it took the school-yard bully to spell it out with brutal unforgettable clarity. Mother never told me anything. Then when my father found out, it took his family a long time to accept me. All my life I've had to fight for anything I wanted."

Nick's expression had turned dark and bitter as he remembered the pain of his childhood. As always, thinking of him suffering as an innocent child affected Amy, even though she knew the story by heart.

Nick's father, Wayne Jackson, was a rancher in south Texas and the king of a million acres scattered around the world. When Wayne had been separated from his wife Mercedes, he'd had a brief affair with Nick's mother, Ticia Browning. By the time Ticia realized she was pregnant, Wayne was reunited with his wife. Nick felt that he'd had to fight his way into the family and battle for acceptance.

Amy turned to face him. "I can't explain. I just can't," she said desperately.

"You mean you won't."

"Why can't you understand that it's too late? Explanations won't make any difference."

He studied her pale, frightened face, and was as puzzled as he always was every time he tried to get to the bottom of what had gone wrong between them. She looked terrified. Of him. Why? That was the question.

"All right. For now," he replied gently, not wanting to push her too far, too soon.

Although Nick had already studied the hodgepodge collection on Triple's shelves, he did so again to give Amy a chance to recover. He felt a heady mixture of fatherly pride and love. Every photograph Nick had ever sent Triple was tacked prominently to his bulletin board. The makeshift gallery was overflowing onto the walls.

There was a jumble of curling yellow articles about Nick's sailing triumphs and glossy color pictures of Nick and his trophies, all dangling at crazy angles from lemon-yellow tacks. He smiled faintly, suddenly reminded that his younger half brother, Jack, had also kept all the pictures and articles about Nick's sailing triumphs just as proudly when they'd been kids.

In many ways Triple reminded Nick of Jack. The boy definitely had Jack's lust for life, his wildness, and Triple was all the more precious to him now that Jack was gone. Triple would need a strong guiding hand, and Amy, for all her dedication, tended to spoil those she mothered.

Nick studied Amy for a minute. "Thank you for letting my son keep all these pictures of me out like this."

"They mean a lot to him," Amy said.

"They mean a lot to me," came that raspy silken tone.

His sincerity caused a warm, wonderful confusion to envelop her.

"There's no reason to thank me," she said stiffly.

His dark gaze narrowed. "You could have turned Triple against me, but you didn't. A lot of women who felt the way you did would have."

"That wouldn't have been the fair thing to do."

"And I'm grateful."

She fought to avoid the blue infinity of his eyes. Instead of looking at him she kept studying the writhing legs in the spiders' jar. "I did it for Triple," she whispered brokenly, "not you. Boys need to be proud of their fathers."

"Perhaps you should amend that to boys need their fathers," he said, his voice dry and sardonic.

"You never miss a chance, do you?"

"I try not to," he said.

Their eyes met and held for an instant, until she looked away.

Nick broke the awkward silence, changing the subject. "Who's been feeding all of Triple's . . . er . . . pets while he's been sick?"

"Probably no one."

"Then I'll take over that responsibility," Nick said. "What do they eat?"

She turned and looked at the beasts scrambling in their jars. She grimaced. "Each other."

Amy had spoken with loathing and disgust, but behind her, Nick burst into laughter. Even as the pleasant sound shivered down her spine, she turned in surprise, intensely conscious of how attractive he was. She couldn't resist a giggle of her own.

Soon the deep rich sounds of their mingled joy filled the room. It was the first time in years that they'd laughed together.

Amy giggled until tears sparkled in her eyes. In his delight, Nick reached out and took her arms, instinctively drawing her close and hugging her. She felt the brush of his jaw and chin against her hair, and an electric current shot through her.

Too late she realized what she had done. She stopped laughing, and so did he, but they continued to cling to each other a little breathlessly. Treacherous sensations of intimacy flowed through Amy. She pressed her hands against his shoulders and arched away from his chest. He let her go, and she backed away clumsily. But the spontaneous moment of shared humor had touched her more than she'd wanted it to. She felt shy and embarrassed. She couldn't stop herself from recalling how delicious it was to be folded against the warmth of Nick's body. It was all too easy to remember how charming and fun loving he could be—too easy to remember how deeply she'd once loved him.

"I'm serious, Nick," she said, trying to be. "They do eat each other, but you'll have to ask Triple who eats who."

Nick lifted a wire-screened box from a shelf to examine it more closely. "What's in here?"

"Careful," Amy said with a shiver. "That's Geronimo."

"Geronimo?"

"Triple's snake," she whispered.

"His cage is practically falling apart," Nick said. "If Geronimo doesn't get a square meal before long, he's going to slip out one of these cracks where the lid's warped."

"At the moment Geronimo is the least of my worries."

"I know what you mean," Nick said gently. "Why don't we call the hospital and check on Triple? If he's okay, we'll eat and rest a bit and then go back."

She didn't resist when he touched her waist possessively, guiding her out of their son's bedroom. It never occurred to her to marvel at how quickly and ruthlessly he was zeroing in on his targets—her heart and soul.

Five

Triple was doing well at the hospital, so Amy and Nick enjoyed a late dinner with Sam. They spread out plates of cold cuts and fruit in the informal dining room that overlooked the Pacific. Lights from the boats offshore flickered against the darkness.

Lorrie had not come home. Amy wondered guiltily if she had sensed Nick would be there and was avoiding him. Ever since Amy had married Nick, Lorrie had been terrified he'd find some way to move in with them.

Sitting across the table from Amy, Nick was stunning. The lapis color of his dress shirt turned his eyes a most dazzling shade of blue. Amy tried not to look at him because every time she did, she felt the warmth of his intense gaze skimming over her, caressing her, and she would quiver in response to this pleasantly disturbing sensation. She would glance down quickly at her plate, but not so quickly that Nick didn't realize how he had affected her. She knew if she glanced up at such a time, she would catch the knowing flash of one of his frequent white smiles.

"I am always delighted by the view in this room," Sam said.

Nick smiled lazily. "So am I."

Sam was looking at the glistening ocean. Nick was watching Amy eat strawberries with her fingers. He seemed to take great pleasure as her white teeth nipped the red skin of the berries and sank delicately into the luscious pink fruit. He smiled every time she licked a pearly droplet of sweet juice from her fingers.

Amy's gaze lifted to his during this sticky process. Nick was regarding her with a gaze of sheer aesthetic appreciation, as if he considered her an opulent masterpiece of female flesh. She had finished licking her fingertips. Her tongue was flicking tidily over her lips, leaving them moist and luminously soft. His eyes grew hot, and his hungry look made her creamy skin glow as pinkly as that of the lush strawberries she'd been nibbling. Embarrassed, she brought her napkin to her lips, hiding the lower part of her face from his view as seductively as a beautiful houri in a Muslim harem. She lowered her long-lashed eyes and ate no more.

His gaze lingered.

After dinner Apolonia served mugs of hot chocolate topped with whipped cream and cups of steaming black coffee.

"Tomorrow morning I go to grocery store and do the shopping, Mr. Nick," Apolonia apologized. "Tomorrow night I serve you hot meal."

Nick beamed at her. "This was wonderful. Especially the strawberries."

Amy blushed, but no one other than Nick saw it. He noticed everything.

Apolonia, who seemed younger and prettier than usual, was chattering gaily. She was wearing a frilly, girlish apron that Amy had never seen before. She had even put on lipstick, and she smiled almost as often as Nick did.

When Apolonia had returned to the kitchen, Sam said to Amy, "It always amazes me how different Apolonia is around Nick. She can be so difficult."

"That's a talent I need to hone in the near future," Nick said carefully, looking at his wife. "There's a certain difficult woman I'm set on charming." Nick's slow tone was laced with sardonic amusement.

A chill settled over Amy. Although she made no comment, she couldn't keep her heart from fluttering, or her senses from stirring.

Time passed uneventfully as they finished dinner. Lorrie did not come home. Nick was unusually quiet. He seemed content to lean back and listen to father and daughter tease one another affectionately. From time to time Amy wondered uneasily what Nick was thinking.

As he watched Sam and Amy, a warmth invaded Nick's soul. Amy's life had always been filled with people, and he'd enjoyed being part of the hubbub when they'd dated. She still lived with her child, her father and her sister. His own life was empty by comparison. For years he'd let himself believe all she'd wanted was money. Now he could no longer justify that shallow assumption he'd made as a sop to his own wounded ego when she'd rejected him as a man. For all her hardness as a businesswoman, Amy had always known how to fill her life with love and people, and although Nick was an extrovert, he didn't.

He'd built himself a beautiful house that overlooked San Francisco Bay, but it was so vast and lonely, he rarely spent time there. He was always flying from city to city alone to check on the far-flung branches of South Sails. He'd been able to throw himself into the America's Cup campaign with a vengeance because it was no sacrifice for him to give himself completely to the effort that cost most men their families. No one cared if Nick Browning sailed fourteen hours a day, seven days a week, month after month, for two to three years.

As Nick watched Amy and Sam, he realized how sick he was of no one caring. Why should he live alone when he had a wife and child? He'd lost a lot of time being angry at Amy for the way she'd used him, but that was over. Maybe she'd wanted his money, but he'd always hungered for the love that permeated her life. Suddenly he was determined to have it again.

After dinner Nick drove Amy to the hospital, and they looked in on their child and found him sleeping peacefully. His progress was so favorable that Nick found it easy to persuade Amy to return home and get a full-night's sleep in her own bed.

It was almost midnight when they returned. Nick seemed to realize how tired she was and let her go to her own room at once.

Alone, Amy quickly took her hair down and changed into an old-fashioned flannel nightgown, buttoning it to her throat. When she heard the jaunty sounds of Nick singing to himself in his own, tuneless, raucous way, she turned on her radio to shut him out. She didn't like dwelling on the unpleasant fact that he'd be sleeping next to her in Triple's bedroom.

Later, sinking into her bed, Amy was so exhausted she expected to fall asleep at once. But she lay awake for hours. It was strange that the night before, in Nick's arms on a narrow couch in a hospital waiting room, sleep had come so easily.

Tonight her thoughts tumbled restlessly over each other. She kept thinking of Nick, recalling how his blue shirt had hugged his lithe body, how his eyes had sparkled every time he'd looked at her from across the table. She remembered his kiss, how his mouth had covered hers in the hospital and how wantonly she'd welcomed his passion. She remembered as well how tenderly they'd laughed together later in their son's room. It was suddenly difficult to remember the terrible reasons why she had to resist him.

She envisioned him standing resplendently naked in Triple's bedroom. She recalled as well their last night together two years before. Nick had been so devastated in his grief, so alone, with none of his family there. Her heart had gone out to him. She'd been so afraid for him. She'd wanted only to ease his pain when she'd welcomed him into her arms, never dreaming she would respond to his touch again. To her amazement she'd found an ecstasy and a thrilling completeness in his lovemaking beyond anything she'd ever imagined. Afterward she'd come frighteningly close to forgiving him. The hardest thing she'd ever done was to leave the next morning and face the loneliness and sorrow of knowing she could never have him.

Never... The word seemed to repeat itself in her weary mind.

Long ago she'd made a promise to Lorrie. Because of it she was now doomed to lead her life separately from Nick's. She had to protect not only herself, but the two people she loved most.

There was no way to go back, to rethink whether what she had done was right or wrong. There were no second chances. The one thing she knew was that she had to get Nick out of her life as soon as possible.

But how? He seemed so determined to stay.

At last Amy threw off her sheets and got up. She pulled on her thick terry robe and stepped out onto her balcony, into the shining darkness.

The night was crisp and cold. A sliver of moon hung in a black and starless sky. She went to the railing and gazed out upon the glistening ocean and the mansions that hugged its edge.

"Guilty conscience?" The low, raspy voice came from behind her, following her train of thought much too closely for comfort.

She started. "I couldn't sleep; that's all."

Nick was lounging against the railing in front of Triple's door. Moonlight outlined his body and she strained to look at him. "Neither could I," he said.

She wanted to rush back into her room, to try to make some sense of her troubled thoughts, but that was out of the question. Nick read her mind, approaching her lazily, cutting off her avenue of escape.

"Beautiful night," he murmured.

"Yes."

His eyes sparkled. "Beautiful woman."

A warm flush ran through Amy, terrifying in its pleasure; a driving physical need, astonishing in its intensity.

"There's something so peaceful about the aftermath of a storm," he said.

She nodded in silent agreement, glad that he didn't seem to expect her to speak.

"Or the aftermath of a lovers' quarrel." The conversation had shifted to a more dangerous topic. "I guess it's a natural pattern—violence followed by a peaceful interlude. Do you remember the way we used to fight?"

Amy remembered all too well. Shifting uneasily, she tried to concentrate on the moon that was blazing in its glory.

"We'd make up, and there would be a beautiful closeness between us," he said softly, dangerously.

She told herself not to listen, but she was drawn by the sound of his voice. His words wove a spell and time seemed to slide backward.

"I remember another night like this one, after a storm, when the ocean was washed with moonlight," he said.

Oh, Amy thought, so did she. Her fingernails dug into the soft wood of the railing as she fought to deny the poignant memory. It was no use. The feelings he'd aroused were overwhelming.

"We were young and in love."

"Nick, don't . . ." she whispered desperately.

"We were sailing Sebastian's *Marauder* offshore when a storm blew up, and we had to seek shelter behind the leeward side of an uninhabited Island."

He said no more, but he didn't have to. What had happened had been wonderful, unforgettable. She'd been a virgin, and she'd never meant to let him make love to her. But he had, and it had been too natural, too beautiful and too perfect to regret. That night had been their beginning. It was only later, after he'd betrayed her and she'd learned how little she'd really meant to him, that she was sorry.

"You don't know how hard I've tried to forget everything about you," she said bitterly.

"No harder than I've tried. There was a time—before Jack's funeral—that I thought I'd succeeded. Now I know I never will. What happened to us, Amy? Why won't you tell me?"

Because the answers to those questions could destroy too many lives, she thought.

"Do you know what's bothered me the most all these years?" he asked.

"I can't imagine."

"When you found out you were pregnant, you didn't come to me."

Amy was suddenly terribly afraid. In the empty chasm of silence, her heart thundered violently.

She heard a sound like a door shutting softly near Lorrie's room. Had she only imagined it?

Amy couldn't look at Nick. She couldn't face him. He found her too easy to read.

"I never understood that," he continued. "You'd always been so open with me. Everything was fine between us until I went away to Berkeley at the end of the summer. You were supposed to come, too, but you didn't. I didn't know what to think. Why did you promise to come as soon as you finished your job as lifeguard if you never meant to? Why didn't you call? Why didn't you come? All you would say was that you'd changed your mind. Amy, why haven't you ever been willing to tell me what happened?"

At first she hadn't wanted to hear anything he had to say, but later, when she'd known for certain about the baby, she'd wanted to. She'd almost gone to him that once, and that mistake had nearly cost her everything. She watched the waves roll against the distant beach and shivered.

If Nick ever discovered that the mother of her son was not Amy but the immature Lorrie, he might find a way to take Triple from her.

"Amy?"

She wanted to turn to him, to tell him everything, but that was something she could never do.

Long ago she'd decided that her only defense with him was silence.

There was only the sound of the surf. And the frightened shuddering of her heart.

At last he spoke again. "When I came back to L.A. to find you, you and Lorrie were gone. No one would tell me where. It wasn't until a year later that Sebastian had a few too many beers after a hard race and accidentally let the cat out of the bag. He told me you had a ten-month-old baby and that he'd been helping you. He let me have it right there in the Riviera Yacht Club bar, practically accusing me of getting you pregnant, of abandoning you. He demanded to know when I was going to make things right between us."

Dear Sebastian, she thought. How could he have known that telling Nick was the worst possible thing he could have done?

"I came to you at once, of course. I'll never forget the look of hate in your eyes when you opened the door with Triple in your arms and saw that it was me. We'd been so careful, it had never occurred to me you might get pregnant. When I asked you if the baby was mine, you didn't have to say anything. The truth was in your eyes. By then you'd already graduated from UCLA with honors on the scholarships Sebastian had helped you get. He'd hired you, so you had no use for me. I know you would have thrown me out, if I hadn't forced my way into the house. Why?"

Amy's eyes were glittering. She spoke softly. "Because it was over between us, Nick. I didn't love you anymore. I just wanted you out of my life."

"But there was more to it than that. I felt it in my gut, just as I feel it now. Amy, I can't live like this anymore—not knowing what went wrong. I want a real marriage."

"Then you should have married someone else."

"But I loved you. And you were the mother of my child. No other woman could have given me that."

She flinched, and her face went even whiter than the moon. Again, her nails scored the railing. "Even so, it was wrong of you to force me to marry you," she managed quietly.

"You should have known I couldn't let Triple grow up illegitimate the way I had—nameless, feeling like he didn't fit in anywhere. He had to know he had a father who loved him—and his mother."

It would be so easy to believe his pretty words. Too easy. It was more difficult to remember how he'd gone away to Berkeley, how he'd called only once to ask her why she hadn't come, how casually he'd seemed to accept her change of plans, how indifferent he'd been until he'd found out about Triple. Perhaps, in his way, he did love her, but her way was not so casual and never so cruel.

"It's over, Nick." A sob caught in her throat. "It's been over for years."

He laughed in the darkness. "That's what you keep telling me. At the moment I can think of only one way to convince you that you're wrong."

He touched her, and she shivered. "What are you so afraid of, Amy?" His fingers ran lightly down her body, reaching inside her terry wrapper and leaving in their wake a quicksilver, tingling awareness of him.

She could have stopped him if he'd been savage, but he wasn't. He was infinitely gentle, and his gentleness beguiled her. She wanted him so much. There was a look in his eyes she'd seen there before, an urgency, a wanting, a desperation. Only tonight his determination burned more fiercely than it ever had in the past.

She felt hot, keenly alive, and in that moment everything that stood between them was as nothing. There was only passion, dark need, desire. He pulled her into his arms, his male hardness pressing into her thighs. His hand slid over her body, caressing her. She moaned softly as she felt herself succumbing to the powerful force of his magnetism. He coiled a black length of her loose hair between his fingers and held her face so close she could feel the warmth of his breath tickle the skin above her mouth.

"You've haunted me, Amy," he muttered in a strange harsh voice. "You'll never know how many times I've imagined you, heavy with my child, desperate and alone. I will never forgive myself for that. Never. Let me make it up to you. Give us a chance, Amy. Maybe you don't love me now, but for God's sake, give us a chance."

She felt a rush of guilt. But he kissed her, and there was a ferocity in him that she had never known. His lips sought to draw her into the vortex of his passion. His kisses seemed to go on endlessly. Her arms encircled his neck. She felt the thunder of his heart as a piercing wild hunger swept through them both.

The moonlight glinted off the water; the salt smell of the ocean enveloped them.

His lips left her mouth, and she felt their heat as he trailed kisses over her cheek into the smooth downy softness of her hairline.

She laid her head against his chest, and her raven hair streamed over his shoulders like a silken veil, wrapping around the bare skin of his throat as the feathery wisps blew on the cool breeze that came off the water. She caught his clean musky scent, and the slow ache that began in the middle of her belly seemed to spread throughout her body.

He pushed the edges of her robe aside, and only thin flannel separated his exploring hands from her body as he caressed her soft belly. His hands slid upward ever so slowly. She heard the catch of his indrawn breath as he found the soft velvet mounds of her breasts and fondled them until their fleshy tips hardened.

"Oh, Amy," he groaned, his callused palms seeking and exploring the warm, yearning womanliness of her.

She sighed and plunged her hands into the glorious thickness of his golden hair, pulling his face and mouth closer again, wanting nothing more than to be consumed by the white heat of his frenzied kisses, by his velvet torrid touching.

His touch alone was splendor and beauty. Never had she wanted any other man. She was glad of the darkness, glad that there was nothing to distract her from the warm, live contact of his mouth against her skin, of his body pressed into hers. He was beauty. And she was beauty. And the whirl of emotion he aroused was beauty.

He continued to kiss her in that mad, wonderful intimate way until she was breathless, until some new nakedness deep within her stirred, and she knew she was opening herself to him again, surrendering not only her body but her soul.

Along with the passion came the sweetness of her love for him, that same dangerous sweetness that had seduced her so many years before. Only she wasn't the naive girl she'd been then. She was a woman who'd known not only the full force of love, but the terrible pain of betrayal.

Her world was spinning out of control. There was only Nick, and her love, and in that moment the wrongness of loving him didn't matter anymore.

A soft moan of pleasure was rising in her throat as he led her toward her bedroom door. She had to open her eyes to find her way. Dimly, far beneath, Amy became aware of a fluttery movement on the beach. A woman with golden hair was walking aimlessly along the water's edge. She was bundled in white furs against the chill, but filmy white skirts swirled around her slender ankles. Rhinestone slippers dangled from her fingers.

The thought flickered in the back of Amy's mind that it was odd for a woman in an evening gown to do such a thing on such a cold night—even in Malibu. She focused her attention on the woman. The wind swept the girl's hair back from a fragile face.

Lorrie! Only Lorrie would do such a thing! Lorrie must have come home. She must have seen them on the balcony together. She had been frightened. Amy realized how extremely upset Lorrie must be to go near the water.

An image from the past rose in Amy's mind: that golden hair matted in seaweed, that delicate face lying white and lifeless in the roiling surf, that body limp and frozen as it was stirred by the waves. "My fault . . ." Amy whispered dully, remembering the agony of that night. "My fault . . ."

Lorrie must have come home tonight and somehow discovered that Nick was here. Amy saw it all so clearly. Lorrie hadn't been able to deal with his presence in the house. She probably thought that Amy had wanted him here, that she'd even asked him here. Lorrie had felt lost and confused. Whenever she felt threatened she went down to the water. It was something she'd done ever since the tragic boating accident, once with near fatal consequences.

Amy pushed anxiously against Nick's shoulders. "You have to stop," she whispered, panic in her low tone. "I can't . . . I just can't."

"What?" His hands on her body tightened. Then he let her go. She could feel his eyes, intense, questioning.

She turned anyway, ashamed that she'd come so close to losing control. Her life and the life of her family had been shattered twice—once by death, once by love. Both times she'd felt terrified by the feeling that there were no rules, no control, that she was helpless to change her destiny.

Never again.

Once she'd made the mistake of loving the same man her sister had loved, and she'd nearly wrecked all of their lives.

She couldn't allow Nick to destroy them all over again.

From some deep reserve of inner strength she summoned the willpower to push him away.

She leaned against the railing feeling dazed and breathless.

All he had to do was touch her again, and she would have been lost.

But he didn't touch her. For a long moment they stared at one another. His face was dark, closed, but the blazing passion in his eyes jolted through her and left her shaken.

"Amy." Nick's voice was low and charged with emotion.

"If you force me tonight, I swear I'll never forgive you," she whispered.

He expelled a long breath of angry frustration. "So what's new?" But he backed away from her, widening the distance between them in order to resist the impulse to drag her into his arms again. "Why, Amy?" he demanded hoarsely. "Why? I'm not leaving until I know."

Lorrie was standing directly beneath them in the shadows. Amy looked from her sister to Nick.

"Why are you so determined to torture me with these questions?" came Amy's sobbing cry. "By making love to me?"

"I don't want to torture you. I want to love you."

"No." She shook her head. The pain splintering through her body was too great to be borne. "You never loved me. You don't even know the meaning of that emotion. You don't love. You only make love," she said, weeping angrily. "And I hate you! Do you understand? I've hated you for years!"

She was shaking, and tears were streaming down her cheeks. Amy Browning never, never, screamed at people. She never cried. Only Nick could shatter the shield of bitter control she hid behind.

Only Nick.

She turned to run. His hand gripped her shoulder to stop her.

"You don't hate me," he taunted softly. His fingers cut into her flesh. "You love me."

She twisted out of his reach and dashed toward the door to her room, slamming it and bolting it once she was inside.

His fist pounded against the glass, but she refused to let him in.

"Go away!" she moaned.

If she opened the door, there would be no stopping him. Wrong! There would be no stopping herself.

She sagged against the wall and hugged her body with her arms. Slowly she sank to the floor and wept bitterly.

For the man she still wanted despite everything.

For the man she must never let herself have.

Six

Amy awoke the next morning feeling even more exhausted than when she'd collapsed on her bed the night before. After she showered, she took great pains to make up her face, attempting to conceal the black circles beneath her eyes. She braided her hair and wound the braids into a sedate knot at the nape of her neck. Then she put on her most severely tailored black suit, a shapeless garment she knew Nick would hate, and headed for the kitchen hoping to drink a cup of coffee before she had to face either him or Lorrie.

On her way she discovered Lorrie's door ajar. Amy pushed it open, calling to her sister softly, but Lorrie was gone. Her bed hadn't even been slept in. Wondering where Lorrie might have spent the night, Amy felt a fresh tug of guilt for having let Nick reenter their lives and cause problems.

Even if Amy could forgive Nick, he would never be accepted by Lorrie. Lorrie had been changed by that night with Nick, and Amy's deep protective feelings for her sister had been outraged. The last thing she wanted to do now was to hurt her. Amy wished that she'd had the strength to go to Lorrie last night and talk to her, but she hadn't been able to.

Amy closed Lorrie's door and hoped that Nick wasn't up, that he hadn't gone down to the kitchen yet.

But he was already there, lounging in one of her kitchen chairs, drinking her coffee, and reading her paper. He was wearing the blue dress shirt that always made his eyes so dazzling. Only this morning, he'd added a navy silk tie.

Sections of newspaper were scattered carelessly across the counters, the table and the chairs. No man messed up a newspaper more thoroughly than Nick.

He was reading the business section, her favorite part of the paper.

He glanced up. She wanted to run. Instead she endured his smile and his sardonic, "Good morning," as if it were the most natural thing in the world for the two of them to share a kitchen.

She felt the cynical blaze of his eyes as he appraised her from the top of her shining black head to the pointed tips of her unfashionable shoes. He let his eyes linger appreciatively in all the wrong places until she flushed. She took a cup down from the cabinet.

He smiled again. "That's got to be the ugliest dress you own."

"I put it on just for you," she retorted, grimacing.

He chuckled. "The urge to rip clothes from your body was never stronger."

Her cup rattled against the blue Formica counter top. "You wouldn't dare!"

Once again his winning grin flashed across his dark face. "Don't tempt me," he murmured, leaning toward her, his brilliant eyes recklessly touching her mouth, her breasts, her thighs. He was a man of lusty, unashamed appetites. With his eyes alone, from across the kitchen, he could devour a woman.

Flames of confusion engulfed her. The white-tiled walls seemed to close in and suffocate her.

Why had she never noticed before how tiny her kitchen was? Or was it that it only seemed so, with his virile presence in the center of it? He dominated the room like a giant golden spider happy to have discovered some hapless creature tangled in its web.

Flustered, she poured herself a cup of coffee.

"You obviously woke up on the wrong side of the bed," he said, his smile broadening.

She found his insolence and cheerfulness equally maddening. "And whose fault is that?"

"Yours entirely, darling. I offered. You refused. Next time..."

"There won't be a next time!" she snapped. "And I'm not in the mood for this sort of conversation."

"But I am. I can't stand a woman who sulks over breakfast. "I'm determined to cheer you up."

"You're not doing a very good job."

"Then I'll have to try harder." His blue eyes danced in merciless merriment.

"Please, just leave me alone."

"That's the last thing I intend to do," taunted his soft, well-modulated voice.

She snatched the business section from him and attempted to read an article, but the words ran together in a blur of tiny black print. She was too vividly aware of that indolent male sprawl of arms and legs across the table, of those avid eyes watching every move she made with excessive interest.

Finally she put the paper down and scowled at him. "I can't concentrate with you staring at me like that."

"There's nothing of interest," he said mildly. His gaze fell to her heaving breasts. "In the paper, I mean."

"This house is too small for the two of us," she whispered feverishly.

"You just haven't gotten used to me," he replied, smiling placidly.

"I don't intend to."

"Then we're at cross-purposes—as usual." The fact didn't seem to bother him in the least.

When she picked up another section of newspaper, he said softly, "I called the hospital."

Instantly her hostility died. Her eyes softened with love and motherly concern. "And?"

"I thought that would get your attention."

"Tell me, damn it!"

"Can you believe Triple's himself again and trying to run the show as he always does. He made them move him out of the intensive care unit this morning. He was eating breakfast when I talked to him and complaining because his cinnamon roll was too mushy. It was all I could do to talk him out of going down to the kitchen and teaching the chef..."

"Oh dear! We've got to get to the hospital," Amy cried, pushing her coffee cup away. "There's nothing more dangerous than Triple unsupervised—when he's not on his deathbed. He can get into trouble faster than any child I've ever known."

"He reminds me of me," Nick said fondly.

"Unfortunately," came her dry retort. "Why couldn't he have been just a little like my side of the family?"

"Maybe when we have a girl," Nick tossed hopefully.

A look of horror flashed across her face. "No..."

Nick merely laughed good-naturedly. "Whenever you're ready, I'll drive you, darling."

She was about to object to this last statement on several points when he pulled her into his arms. His hands plunged into her hair. She could feel his fingers quickly, deftly, unpinning the thick braids looped at her neck.

"What are you doing?"

"Improving the scenery," came his husky tone. Her hair fell in showers of black silk down her shoulders. Gently he ran his fingers through it. "There, that's better."

"Nick, you have no right..."

He gave her a searing look as he undid the top button of her blouse.

"Don't remind me of my rights, honey, unless you want me to exercise a few of them."

Her senses rocked in alarm as she felt the full power of his earthy appeal. "No," she protested raggedly.

Ever so gently he brushed the leaping pulse in her throat with a callused fingertip, and beneath the velvet warmth of this most casual touch, her heart beat all the faster. "Just be glad I don't have time to strip you, darling," he whispered.

"Don't call me—"

"I keep forgetting, darling," he said.

His fingertip remained on her throat. He stared down at her intimately, impertinently, but instead of the fury she wanted to feel, she felt herself melting. Nevertheless, she managed a stern tone. "You're impossible!"

"Like our son. You love him. Why can't you love me?"

For a breathless eternity they stared into one another's eyes. Then his long fingers wound into her thick hair, pulling her head back so that the curve of her slender neck was exposed. Like one mesmerized, Amy watched the slow descent of his mouth. In a dream she felt the light caress of his lips graze hers, and she tasted the flavor of his tongue as it met her own.

Their mouths parted.

"I love you, Amy. I always have, and I always will."

She didn't want to believe him. She couldn't let herself. Nevertheless, her fingers came up and curled around his collar, among the golden tendrils of his hair, and she kissed him back.

Abruptly he released her. For a long moment she kept her eyes closed. At first because she was too stupefied with pleasure to do otherwise. Then, because she was too mortified to face him.

When at last she let them flutter open, she found to her surprise that Nick seemed almost as stupefied as she.

He had been watching her covertly, a look of wonder on his dark face. Then, when she opened her eyes, an impenetrable mask came over his features as if he could not allow himself to believe the emotion he thought he'd read in her languorous expression.

He grabbed her hand and said in a low harsh tone, "Why don't we go?"

When he went to get the car, Amy phoned Triple to make sure he was all right and to give him orders not to get out of bed. Much to her surprise, Lorrie answered.

Amy felt a deep relief to know her sister was safe.

"Lorrie, what are you doing at the hospital?" Amy asked gently.

"I was worried about Triple. You were home...with Nick."

Amy knew it wasn't deliberate, but Lorrie's soft voice lacerated Amy's conscience.

"It isn't like you think..."

Silence.

"Lorrie, I'm sorry."

Silence.

"Please say something," Amy pleaded desperately. "Can you tell me at least if Triple's okay?"

Lorrie hesitated and then began in her weakest voice. "He doesn't even seem sick. He wants me to take him down to the kitchen so he can complain about his breakfast."

"Lorrie, please, you don't have to worry about Nick. He won't be around that long. He only came because of Triple. Just don't let Triple out of your sight. I'm on my way. We can talk when..."

"I don't want to talk."

The line went dead.

When Nick and Amy opened the door to Triple's hospital room, Nick stared in horror at Triple's empty room.

Amy felt only mildly dismayed. She should have known Lorrie couldn't keep Triple here. Lorrie was always putty in the boy's hands. Even at six, his was a strong, fully developed personality, and he knew exactly how to turn an adult's weakness to his own advantage.

"Looks like our little monster's been busy," Amy said, "and I see Lorrie brought him a present from the gift shop."

"Why do you say that?"

"Look!"

Amy pointed to the bright bits of blue foil and streamers of white satin ribbon littering the chairs, the floor, and the bed. In one corner a demolished cardboard box lay askew.

Amy knelt and investigated the torn box. It appeared to have been ripped open by an explosion and then to have belched tiny cars and trucks everywhere.

Nick picked up a discarded miniature red Porsche that had rolled under the bed and set it on the nightstand beside what was left of a half-eaten cinnamon roll.

Other than stuffed animals, Triple had never taken the slightest interest in most toys, a fact Lorrie had never been observant enough to have noticed.

"Where do you think he is?" Nick asked.

"Wherever he can get into the most trouble the quickest," Amy said calmly, sinking into a chair and relaxing for the first time in days. "Lorrie has obviously been as careless as usual and turned her back on him. I wish that could have been avoided, but if Triple is strong enough to seek mischief, he's definitely on the mend."

"We've got to find him," Nick said, alarmed. "Anything could happen to him. Night before last he was at death's door."

"Save your concern for the unlucky person Triple decides to pester."

"How can you be so sure he's all right?" Nick demanded.

"Experience." At Nick's blank look of shock, Amy gave a faint smile. "Never mind. Before long, there will be such a hue and cry that the proper authorities will find him."

Nick paced the room. At every sound in the hall, he would rush to the door. "I don't know how you can take this so coolly," he said.

"I got used to things like this years ago. You forget Triple is not a typical six-year-old. Believe me, the hapless souls who are forced to participate in his adventures are always anxious to return him."

"I can't just stay here and wait. I've got to try to find him."

"Suit yourself," Amy said, closing her eyes. "Why don't you check the kitchen first?"

Nick hadn't been gone long when an army of tight-lipped nurses marched purposefully into the room. At the head of this formidable battalion, Triple was being pushed in a wheelchair. His demeanor was as imperious as that of an Oriental potentate being carried on a litter by an escort of slaves. He was clearly in charge. In each of his hands he tightly clutched two large jars, as if he considered them treasures of vast worth. Several of the nurses were also carrying jars, which they quickly set down on the nearest window ledge seeming only too happy to be rid of them.

Although he looked white-faced and thin, Triple's high-pitched voice rang as exuberantly as usual.

"Mom, I saw a baby being born!"

"You should see what he's done to the kitchen," said one of the nurses.

Amy took this information as calmly as she usually did when faced with one of Triple's adventures. "What were you doing out of your room, dear?"

"No one told me I was supposed to stay in it, Mom."

"You were," Amy said firmly. "I specifically told your Aunt Lorrie..."

"She had to make a phone call."

Amy removed the jars from his hands so the nurses could help him back to bed. In the jars, gray spongy objects hung suspended in formaldehyde.

"What are these, anyway?" Amy asked, setting the disgusting jars in the window.

"Oh, just some tonsils and an appendix a couple of guys had cut out and..."

"I see," Amy said. "Where did you get them?"

"A doctor gave them to me."

"Oh, he did." She helped her son into bed.

"He said I could have them if I'd promise to stay in my room and look at them. Hey, Mom, was he really supposed to spank the baby and make her scream like that? He turned purple when I asked him that. Mom, did it hurt like that when you had me?"

Amy reddened. "Let's not talk about babies right now."

"Mom . . ."

"Never mind, dear. You're not nearly as strong as you think you are. Why don't you lie back and put your head on the pillow?"

A breathless Nick stumbled into the room. His tie swung from his collar at a rakish angle. A lock of golden hair fell across his brow. Amy imagined him racing down miles and miles of hospital corridors. Nick looked even more worried than he had when he'd dashed off to find Triple. "I couldn't find him anywhere."

"That's because I'm right here, Dad," Triple chirped from the bed.

"Triple!" Nick gave a shout and ran to his bed. "Are you okay, son?"

"I saw a baby . . ."

"No more about that baby, Triple," Amy said sternly.

"Okay, Mom." Triple grinned so guilelessly that Amy was immediately suspicious of his intentions.

After the nurses left, Triple lay against the pillow looking pale and exhausted. His eyelids drooped, and sitting beside him quietly, Amy knew he'd soon be asleep.

"Did you spend the night at home, Dad?" Triple murmured.

"I slept in your room, son."

"My room, huh? Right next to Mom's?" Triple grinned wanly. "It was almost worth getting sick so we could be a real family."

A real family. The thought hovered in Amy's mind like an elusive, tantalizing dream before it trailed away. Amy's eyes met Nick's for a charged moment that seemed an infinity. His eyes were shining with an intense emotion she couldn't read. Quickly she looked away, determined to break the spell.

Reluctantly Nick turned back to Triple. "Son, don't you go having any harebrained ideas about not getting well—just to keep me here." His voice was husky, and his eyes were disarmingly gentle as they slid from his son's to Amy's face. "Nothing anyone can do or say is going to drive me away again."

Amy stared at him wordlessly as his hand covered hers. She didn't pull away as his callused thumb caressed the soft inner flesh of her palm.

The hospital door opened and closed, allowing a beautiful blonde dressed in white silk, white fur, and white rhinestones to sweep inside on a breath of perfume.

"Hi, Aunt Lorrie."

Lorrie looked ethereal, like a figment from a dream.

Amy and Nick sprang apart instantly. Amy's face darkened guiltily. Nick looked annoyed.

Lorrie ignored Triple's greeting. She ignored her sister as well. "Hello, Nick," she said softly, attempting to bridge the awkwardness. "A-Amy...told me you were here."

Nick glanced toward Lorrie with a look of cool indifference, and a white-faced Lorrie dropped her eyes.

Nick saw Amy's stricken expression. She was staring dazedly at him. When the seconds ticked by and no one spoke, Lorrie tried to cover the awkward moment by talking about her acting career. All she did was make Nick more aware that something was wrong.

For the next half hour, while Lorrie spoke of her latest audition for a television sitcom, Nick was acutely aware of Amy's subtle change of mood. She seemed tired, drained, depleted, curiously on edge, and he was at a loss to understand why. In the past Amy had always adored her younger sister to a fault and been overly protective of her.

Amy seemed to retreat within herself. It was almost as if she weren't there, and he was alone in the room with Lorrie and Triple.

"Well, it's time I went. I just had to come by and check on you, Triple," Lorrie said, patting Triple's hand and clinging to it. "You know how special you are to me since I'll never be able..." Lorrie's voice broke.

Triple's eyes were closed. He was pretending to be asleep. Nick, who'd been studying his wife and only half listening, saw Amy whiten with pain.

"You see, Nick," Lorrie said. "A few years ago, shortly after you left, I was ill. So ill, I'll never be able to have a baby of my own. Triple's all I have."

Nick was watching Amy, who looked utterly bleak.

"I'm sorry," Nick said quietly.

Amy pressed her eyes tightly shut and turned away. "I...I think I'll leave you two to watch Triple for a while," she said, her low voice curt with repressed pain.

"I'll go with you," Nick offered.

"No!" Amy turned wildly, refusing to so much as look at either of them. "I have to be alone!" She stumbled toward the door. "You belong here, Nick. With Lorrie and Triple."

Nick would have rushed after her, if Lorrie hadn't stopped him. "Can't you see she doesn't want you?"

"Hell, yes, I see." He felt impatient, on the verge of something momentous, and Lorrie was deliberately detaining him. "I've got to go after her," he snapped. "I've got to find out what's wrong."

"Let her go, Nick," Lorrie said softly. "Haven't you hurt her enough?"

"All I ever wanted to do was love her. Maybe I made a few mistakes along the way..."

Lorrie blanched.

She opened her mouth, but he didn't wait for her reply. "Watch Triple a minute, will you? Only this time do something right for a change and really watch him." He spun on his heel and was gone.

Though he searched everywhere, Nick couldn't find Amy. She had chosen her hiding place too well. Nor could he force her to tell him what was wrong when she returned to Triple's room hours later.

It was as if her heart and soul had turned to ice.

She was colder to Nick than she'd ever been before.

Amy sat rigidly at her desk, scribbling notes as fast as she could, which wasn't fast enough because Sebastian was barking orders over the phone at an even faster rate.

Two uneventful days had passed since Triple had run loose in the hospital. Since that time, Amy and Nick had taken turns staying with him.

This strategy had been Amy's idea. She liked it because it served a double purpose. Not only was Triple supervised, but she didn't have to see Nick except for the few minutes their shifts overlapped.

Thus there had been no more sticky moonlit conversations, no more sharing of her kitchen and her morning newspaper with him, and no more having to watch Lorrie and him together.

Today Triple was coming home from the hospital.

Today Nick had to leave—for good; before he became firmly entrenched; before he became set on staying forever!

Nick had gone to pick up Triple from the hospital. Amy had planned to go with him, but Sebastian had called, and Sam had offered to go in her place.

Sebastian continued shouting in his excitement. "Of all the times for that kid of yours to pull one of his stunts, this is the absolute worst!"

"I don't usually defend Triple, but not even he could help getting sick, Sebastian."

"Maybe not, but you have to admit drama stalks that kid. I need you, Amy! I don't know the first thing about running Crackle!"

Sebastian was upset because he'd followed one of Amy's hunches and caught two of his key executives embezzling at his potato-chip factory at Long Beach and fired them.

"It's your company."

"One of many, and one I hired you to take care of. I've been here all week. I feel like I'm drowning in potato chips! I can't give you another day off! You've got to be on the premises until you can find someone to replace those two weasels, Beashel and Sheldon. I leave in two days to close that land deal in Australia."

"Then you could give me at least one more day. Triple—"

"Triple's fine. I checked on him myself yesterday. Nick was there. He and the doctor told me Triple's recovery verges on the miraculous. Once that kid's home, he'll be tearing the place apart in no time."

"That's what I'm afraid of. Apolonia's down with the flu again. She went out in the garden during the storm. Sam's not up to chasing Triple."

"Then let Nick chase him! He's offered to."

"He what?"

"And I accepted his generous offer—on your behalf, naturally. He seemed so thrilled, I was touched. So was Triple, for that matter. If you were smart, you'd be thrilled, too. Forgive Nick. Use this opportunity to—"

"Sebastian!"

For all his outward gruffness, Sebastian was an incurable romantic.

"You know I'm right."

"Sebastian, you're meddling in my life—"

"No. I'm merely putting my own affairs in order. I'm going to Australia. You're going to work. Nick stays, and that's final!"

With that, he hung up. For a long moment Amy stared out the window, weighing her options.

There weren't many.

It would do no good to call Sebastian again. He never backed down once he'd made a decision. She tried to think of just one baby-sitter she could call, but all the good ones had told her not to call again.

Nevertheless, she was determined about one thing. Nick was not staying.

The front door banged open with such a violent thud that the whole house shook. Triple's shout reverberated off the tile floors and redwood ceilings.

"Mom!"

She heard the sound of shattering glass.

"I'm coming, dear." She rushed down the hall toward the front door to find a remorseful Triple studying the fragments of a crystal ashtray.

"I bumped into it by accident. Honest, Mom."

He looked so troubled, her heart went out to him. "Never mind, dear."

Triple threw himself into her arms. "Guess what?"

She looked down at him, the ashtray forgotten. A tender smile tugged the corners of her lips.

"Dad says he's staying! For a whole week! Till I get really well! And look what he got me!"

In one hand Triple was holding an immense toy sailboat that was almost as tall as he was. An antenna was attached to the tip of its mast. "He's going to use it to teach me to sail."

"Triple, you've been very sick. I'm not about to let you near the water."

Triple was starting to protest when Nick and Sam came through the door together. Nick was laden down with suitcases and a huge stuffed gorilla he had given Triple as a gift. Sam was carrying the rest of his grandson's possessions. They were laughing over some bit of shared humor.

"Private joke?" Amy asked.

"I was just saying I never saw a hospital process a bill faster," Nick replied. "Triple certainly made a name for himself."

"That was a fun place," Triple said.

"Triple, why don't you take your boat and gorilla and go to your room and lie down?" Amy said, determined to talk to Nick alone.

"I will . . ." Triple glanced earnestly at his mother. "But only if you promise not to make Dad go."

"Triple!"

"Go on, son," Nick said.

Triple squared his jaw mutinously, exactly as Nick did when he was determined to have his own way. Then he ran to his father.

"Don't worry, son," Nick said softly, rumpling the tawny curls. "I can handle your mother."

Triple regarded his father dubiously and remained where he was.

Nick's blazing blue eyes met hers. Amy felt acutely uncomfortable. Still, she managed to speak gently. "I'd really like to thank you for all you've done the past few days, Nick."

"You're welcome," he said, his voice as deceptively soft as hers.

"But, I really think that since Triple's home now, and so much better, we don't need to impose on you any longer."

"Believe me, it's no imposition," Nick replied in that same silken tone.

"I'm sure you must be worried about South Sails," Amy persisted.

"Why? I've been in touch with the office every day. I have complete faith in my staff. If you hire the right team, a company will run itself.

She sent a small, forced smile in his direction. "How very fortunate," she retorted.

His gaze narrowed. "Yes, isn't it?"

"What I was trying to say, Nick, is that you must have a million important things to do."

"I do. You and Triple head the list."

"Why must you always be deliberately obtuse?" she muttered.

There was a watchful stillness in his expression. "Is it so wrong of me to want to help my wife and son when they need me?"

A frown of exasperation swept across her brow. "But we don't need you! Dad can look after Triple."

Sam had listened thus far in silence, but he shook his white head in vigorous dismay at the idea of baby-sitting Triple full time.

"Dad, please..."

"I suppose I could do all right if I had Nick here to back me up," Sam said at last in a conspiratorial tone.

"Dad, Lorrie can help out," Amy pleaded.

"Honey, you know as well as I do that when Lorrie helps she only makes things more difficult. It's best not to count on her for much."

Amy stared hard at her son, her husband, and her father. Never had three male faces been set in more stubborn lines. She couldn't fight them all.

"Mom, he can stay in my room." Triple's eyes were shining with hope.

"He can bunk in with me," Sam countered with equal enthusiasm.

All eyes focused on her, as if everyone expected her to invite Nick into her bedroom, and Amy blushed.

"Oh, that won't be necessary," Nick replied grandly, having prolonged the embarrassing moment as long as possible. "I'll just move my suitcase into that little guest room off the garage. I don't expect to share a room...or a bed...with anyone." He was staring pointedly at his wife.

Nick was enjoying himself. The devil, she thought furiously, for having put her in such a difficult position. But how could she break Triple's heart or disappoint her father after all they'd been through? Triple's recovery was truly miraculous, and she didn't want to do anything that might risk complications.

"Then it's settled," Nick declared triumphantly. "I'm staying. At least for a week." His brilliant eyes touched hers. "Maybe even longer."

"Oh, boy!" Triple cried. "Thanks, Mom."

Triple threw himself into her arms and hugged her.

Glad as she was to have her little boy safely home once more, Amy could feel nothing but horror at the insurrection taking place in her own household.

Nick moved closer and put his arm around Triple and Amy.

She glanced up, seeking Nick's eyes. His fingers tightened on her body, and she shivered.

An undercurrent of electricity flowed between them, its tingling existence such a tangible truth, there was no way to ignore it.

"You won't be sorry," Nick whispered over Triple's head, smiling at her in that way of his that made her feel, despite everything she knew to be true, that she was the only woman in the world for him.

His gaze zeroed in on her parted lips. "I think this calls for a kiss—to seal our bargain, so to speak," he murmured.

She was blinded by the dazzling light in his eyes.

"No..." She reeled away, swallowing convulsively, afraid for him to see how shaken she was.

Trembling, she clung to Triple.

She heard the velvet resonance of Nick's voice. "Soon," he murmured. "Soon." His tenderness reached out and seemed to enfold her with his warmth. "We have a week."

Amy lowered her dark eyes to the tousled gold-brown head of the son they both held in their arms.

She knew suddenly that the most horrible thing of all was the insurrection in her own heart.

Seven

The glass doors to the swimming pool stood open when Amy came downstairs three days later. She knew what those open doors meant, and a painful pulse beat low in her stomach.

Triple and his father were already up, practicing sailing techniques with the remote-control, miniature twelve-meter Nick had given Triple.

Dear Lord! How was it possible that Nick had fit into her life so easily and smoothly? Like Triple, Nick had boundless energy, and he'd made himself incredibly useful. If he wasn't playing chess with Sam or nursing Apolonia, or singing those raucous tuneless songs of his while he cooked in the kitchen, Nick was entertaining Triple by the hour. Only Lorrie was upset by Nick's presence, so upset she'd packed a bag and gone to stay with a friend until he left. Not that her defection seemed to bother Nick or anyone else, except Amy.

Nick was too busy teaching his son sailing theory and chess, helping him learn to read, and helping him care for his pets. Last night, Triple's discovery that Geronimo had slithered out of his poorly constructed cage, Nick had shown Triple how to make the necessary repairs to the screened box, just in case they found the snake.

Father and son were inseparable, and it bothered Amy that Triple had become so emotionally dependent on his father. It was going to break Triple's heart when Nick had to go.

Though she knew she should grab a cup of coffee and hit the freeways before rush hour, Amy was too curious to pass the doors without peeping inside. She stopped, edging cautiously toward the shadowed doorway so they wouldn't notice her.

Near the diving board Nick had positioned a huge fan to simulate wind. He could roll the fan to different spots whenever he desired a new wind direction. Every day father and son practiced for hours with the boat.

Inside the room, the air was warm and dense with humidity and the scent of chlorine. Sunlight glittered on the dancing water of the pool.

Triple was reclining in a chaise lounge, his head propped against a mound of plump red pillows, the little boat's remote-control device clutched tightly in one fist. Nick's giant golden form was crouched beside him, and Nick was whispering instructions and helpful comments. As always Amy marveled that such an impatient man could be so patient with a child.

Triple was listening to his father with such rapt attention that he wasn't watching the sailboat. Suddenly the twelve-meter hit a gust from the fan and lurched saucily, its sails dipping into the water, and its bow ramming the side of the pool at maximum speed. Triple gave a yelp of rage that was so loud it shook the glass walls. Then he jumped up, raced to the edge, and yanked the boat that had been drifting helplessly on its side out of the glimmering waters and examined the damage.

"Dumb boat! What did it do that for?" he bellowed.

For a minute Amy thought he would throw it.

Then she heard Nick's low soothing voice. "We all make mistakes, son. The thing we have to do is learn from them. You've got to figure out what you did wrong and take corrective measures."

The wind chose that moment to snap the open door against the glass wall where Amy was standing. Nick glanced up, and when he saw her, a wistful expression passed fleetingly over his dark face.

His eyes held hers, and her stomach went weightless as he murmured, "Believe me, son, I've made a mistake I'd give my life to straighten out."

Amy knew that this last remark was meant solely for her, and she was moved by it—much more than she wanted to be.

Nick rose slowly to his full height. As usual he was costumed outrageously. This morning he wore a flamboyantly flowered Hawaiian ensemble that made his skin seem darker and his eyes more brilliant. In the morning sunlight, his thick hair was wispy, spun silver and gold as the fan tossed it back and forth across his brow. His bronzed thighs were thrust widely apart, and in his swimming trunks and unbuttoned tropical shirt, he looked boldly piratical.

Amy felt the blue blaze of his eager gaze roaming across her shapely length as surely as if he had touched her. She wanted to run, but she stood transfixed. The heat of her blood rose as that treacherous part of her nature that found him irresistible flared to life.

She turned blindly, bent on escape, but his deep resonant drawl stopped her.

"Amy, why don't you stay for a minute, so Triple can show you what he's learned?"

Amy glanced away wildly. The blue Pacific stretched placidly toward the horizon. Palm fronds danced lazily in the light winter breezes. Surely there was no danger in such a peaceful setting.

Triple was looking at her, his eyes bright and expectant. "Hey, Mom, watch this!" Triple leaned over, eagerly replacing the boat in the water and nudging it gently into the middle of the pool.

More than anything, she wanted to stay.

"I have to go to work," she said in a tight, constricted voice.

"It'll only take a second, Mom."

As she turned and began to retreat silently down the stairs, she heard a whispered curse. She was aware of Nick's rapid footsteps clamoring behind her.

She stopped. It was no use trying to run from him. Her white-knuckled fingers gripped the railing as he caught up to her.

They were outside, near sugar-white dunes in the brilliant glare of the morning sunshine with its fresh smells and sounds of the sea.

They were alone, where Triple couldn't see them.

"Why won't you stay?" Nick demanded.

She clung even more tightly to the banister. Her head whipped around defiantly, and there Nick was, closer than she'd realized, with his golden, windblown hair and his incredible blue eyes. His loose shirt whipped about him, and a great deal of his hard-muscled chest was revealed.

"You just can't take no for an answer, can you?" Her voice was as thin as a thread.

His hand closed over her shoulder, and he backed her against the railing until its round edge bit into her hip. His own large body loomed against hers.

"You didn't answer my question," he insisted softly. The warmth of his breath slid against her throat like a sensuous caress. "Why won't you watch?"

She felt the darkly veiled intensity of his gaze scanning her face—searching for something.

"Because if I come in," she began, "if I watch you together, it would seem too much like we're a real family."

Blue eyes bored into hers. "That's what we are."

Something in his low voice mesmerized her.

"No," she cried. "And we can't ever be! I don't want Triple to get the wrong idea."

Nick's hand tightened on her shoulder. He moved a half step closer. She had to leave, but there was no way she could, caught as she was between the flimsy banister and the blistering warmth of his body.

She could smell his scent, the mixture of salt and sea combining with the tangy smell of his skin. It was his habit to jog every morning along the beach, work out, and then swim laps in the pool.

"Maybe it's you who has the wrong idea," he murmured huskily. Nick's hand stole around her waist, drawing her into the shelter of his chest and arm. His lips moved down to the hollow beneath her jaw and whispered near her ear, "If we didn't feel so right together, I don't think you'd be half as afraid as you are."

"I'm not afraid."

He studied her shadowed face with its downcast trembling eyes, its half-parted, trembling lips. His hand skimmed the satin softness of her cheek, and her pulse leaped erratically.

"Oh, yes you are." His voice had grown softer. It was the tone he used with women, and some intimacy in his low gravelly voice seeped inside her. A callused fingertip trailed across her quivering mouth.

"You think you're so smart," she cried desperately.

"I know about some things," he murmured.

"Such as?"

"You." A long pause while his eyes studied her. "And me."

She brought up her hand to push him away, but it inadvertently touched his chest, uncovered by his blowing shirt. She felt the bristly whorls of bleached gold that formed a gilded cloud against the darker bronze of his chest. His skin was smooth and warm beneath her fingers.

Her eyes rose to his face. His tanned features were expressionless. His inscrutable gaze met her faltering one. Something electric passed between them.

She knew she should pull her hand away. When instead she let it stay, she realized she was losing the fierce inward battle against the physical arousal of her senses.

A hoarse sob clogged her throat. "I don't like Triple's becoming so emotionally dependent on you."

"Is that so wrong?" he said gently. "After all, I am his father."

"But you'll be leaving soon."

To that Nick said nothing. The intense emotion in his eyes alone spoke to her heart.

"Why can't you see?" she began. "He's always worshiped you from afar. Now you're using his adoration to make him think you can be a part of his life you can never be."

"I don't use people," Nick muttered, letting her go and turning away from her in anger. "That's your specialty, remember?"

She whitened. "Maybe you aren't doing it on purpose," she whispered at last, "but can't you see that if Triple's so thrilled to have you around now, he'll be equally miserable when you leave? Nick, I've been watching him. I can see how hard he's trying to change for you. He'll do anything to please you, even things he normally hates."

"If only his mother were more like him." Nick's smooth tone and quick white smile had their customary devastating impact on her senses.

"Damn you," she whispered.

"Is it so bad that Triple wants to please me?" Nick demanded.

"If he's on his best behavior just because he's hoping to maneuver things so you end up staying, what's going to happen when you leave?"

"Look, all I'm trying to do is make the most of the time I have with him." Nick hesitated. "Triple hates reading and spelling. You told me you frustrate him when you try to help him, but I've got him working happily on those two for an hour every day. Since I have dyslexia myself, I have a deeper understanding of the problem than you; therefore, it's easier for me to help him. I used to help Jack the same way."

"Nick..."

"Has it ever occurred to you that I can give things to Triple you can never give him, just as you can help him in ways I can't? That by keeping me out of his life, you're cheating him? Have you ever wondered why he's always been such a little hellion? Has it ever occurred to you he's starving for something he's not getting—my attention? You're too soft with him, Amy. He needs a firm hand. You spoil him, exactly like you've always spoiled Lorrie. Have you noticed that he hasn't pulled one of his stunts in the last three days? He needs a father to relate to full-time, not just one month out of the year."

Every word Nick spoke was tearing her apart.

"Amy, I love Triple just as much as you do. That's all I'm trying to say. Why is that so wrong?"

A dark, overpowering emotion filled her. "Because... your love was the most destructive force I've ever encountered. Because..." Sunlight glistened in the swirling surf. Amy stopped herself, stunned. The answer had been on the tip of her tongue.

She whirled away. She couldn't explain—ever. She owed Nicholas Browning nothing.

"Triple needs me," Nick said. "You're asking me to neglect my own son, and that's something I won't do—even for you."

She clenched her hands tightly together. She agreed in part, and it upset her that she could agree with him about something so important. Triple was starved for a man's attention. Why hadn't she anticipated that as Triple grew up he would want a father? It was just that she had been so busy going to school, being a mother, and getting ahead in her career that she hadn't taken the time for men.

"You need a man in your life, too," Nick said softly. "I think you crave a man's affection and love just as desperately as Triple does. Amy, you spoil everyone you love. Why won't you let me spoil you?"

He started to touch her. She had been looking at the beach. With a moan she jerked away. "No!"

He stood stock-still, his handsome face dark with hurt.

A muted cry of pain sprang from her soul, only to die on her lips.

His golden hair blew carelessly across his dark brow; his blue eyes were bleak with pain.

Oh, why did he have to be built like a god? With an almost physical ache she remembered what it was to know his hands on her, his lips caressing hers.

A part of her felt like weeping hysterically. Never had she been more tempted to give in to the powerful feelings he evoked.

She must not think of him like that, she told herself angrily.

"Yes," she whispered, "I do need a man, but it can't be you. Never you. You belong to a past I have to bury forever. All I'll ever want from you is a . . . a divorce."

The word seemed to echo in the hushed silence. His dark face turned ashen, and Amy's blood froze in her veins. What had she said? Her heart throbbed dully with numb stupefied pain.

"A divorce! The hell you say!" Nick whispered. His eyes narrowed to slits of cold blue steel as he lunged for her and snapped her against his hard body as if she were nothing. "That's the last thing you'll ever get from me."

"How can you stop me?"

"Don't ask a question like that unless you want the answer," he said roughly, winding his hands in her hair, and yanking her head back so abruptly that a shower of pins rained onto the stairs.

She fought to twist away from the cruel hands that tugged at her hair, from the cruel mouth that descended toward hers. "Can't you see, I have to get on with my own life," she pleaded, frantic. "It's time I gave Triple a father. It's time I found a real husband."

"You have a real husband." A bitter, uncontrolled fury swept over Nick, and he forced her body harder against his own. "Is this real enough for you?" he mumbled thickly. His callused hands positioned her female body intimately against his own hardening male shape.

She gasped as she realized the extent of his arousal. For the briefest second his gaze skimmed the pleading softness of her white face, the terror in her huge eyes and trembling mouth. Tenderness flickered across his face and was gone. Then she shut her eyes helplessly as his lips claimed hers in a hard and brutal kiss.

With his mouth and body he made her his. Hotly he fused their lips together, their bodies, their souls until there was no part of her that did not belong to him. No part of her that did not yearn for him. He kissed her lips, her face, her earlobes, her slender throat, until she was panting and breathless. She was filled with the scent and taste of him. Her blood turned to fire. She felt dizzy, drugged.

"Mom! Dad!" Triple shouted impatiently from the pool.

Slowly, reluctantly, Nick released her. He raked his hands through his hair to smooth it. He fought to control his ragged breathing.

Near faint with desire, Amy sagged wearily against the railing and let the cool ocean breezes fan the long, mussed black waves of her hair.

"Mom!"

Amy couldn't look at Nick. She could feel her pulse pounding in her throat. She felt bruised, shamed. Wanton. Her every impulse directed her to escape quickly.

"Come back and watch him, Amy," Nick said quietly. "I swear I won't bother you again if you do." There was a note of desperate hopelessness in his low, hoarse voice. "Just for a minute," he said. "Whatever I did a moment ago, there's still nothing wrong about a little boy loving both his parents. There's nothing wrong with us taking pride in his accomplishments together. It's something he needs. It's something I want very much to give him."

Hearing it put like that, no matter how much she wanted to, Amy could not say no.

"All right," she agreed softly.

"Thank you." Nick took her hand and pressed it tightly in his as he led her inside. "And Amy?"

"What?" The single word was barely audible.

"No divorce." Passion blazed from his eyes. "Never, between us."

She walked blindly through the glass doors. The small boat was skimming up and down across turquoise waters in a series of zigzag maneuvers, executing one successful tack after the other, but Amy did not see it.

"Watch that, Mom!" Triple shouted. She tried, but her vision was too blurred. "I never would have learned that without Dad. Gosh, it's great having Dad home, isn't it?"

She felt Nick's eyes on her, watching her, waiting for her answer.

Her vision went even blurrier. Her throat was as dry as dust.

"What happened to your hair, Mom?"

"The wind," she muttered even as she felt the telltale color staining her cheeks.

Triple cocked his head inquisitively. "I like it," he said. "It makes you look pretty. I think you're just as glad Dad's home as I am."

Father and son were both looking at her. She tried to speak, but she couldn't. Some emotion that she did not want and would not name had entered her heart, crushing her with its intensity, suffocating her, consuming her in its flame.

After that morning at the pool, Amy worked very hard to avoid Nick, but he worked just as hard to make that impossible. He made her feel that she was fighting a war of wills in her own home, a war that she was losing. Although this far Lorrie had avoided him, he had won her father's, her son's, and Apolonia's allegiances. Thus, if Nick was not working directly on her, one of his confederates was. They loved Nick as passionately as she was determined to despise him, and they wanted him to stay—permanently. They did not understand why he couldn't, and she could not explain. They did not understand that hers was a house of carefully guarded secrets, and it was too dangerous to have Nick around trying to unlock its mysteries. He had to go, and quickly.

One evening after work Amy became upset when she caught Nick browsing through her photograph albums. He was in the den, his golden head bent over an open page. The cabinet doors behind him stood ajar, and the shelves were empty. One glance at the orderly stacks of loose pictures and the mountain of albums littering the sofa and carpet made Amy's blood run cold. He had been going through them all!

Wondering what he was about, she tiptoed stealthily into the room and peered over his shoulder.

Dear Lord! A painful sigh escaped her as she glimpsed an all-too-familiar enlargement of Jack and Lorrie and herself. That picture alone instantly brought back the fateful summer that had almost ruined the lives of everyone Amy loved.

Amy's breath caught at the sight of Lorrie in her gold bikini. Jack and Lorrie were locked in a torrid embrace while anxious big-sister Amy looked on. It was funny how much older and more sophisticated than Amy the glamorous Lorrie, who'd only been sixteen at the time, looked. Nick had snapped the picture and given it to Amy, and across the bottom edge he'd scrawled playfully, "Bet you're frowning 'cause you want to be kissed like that! Anytime..."

Amy fought against a flash of bitter memories. Oh, how she wished she'd been strong enough to resist dating him. Maybe... It had been her fault, everything that happened.

Amy grabbed the album from him and shut it. The last thing she wanted to remember was that summer.

"I should have torn that picture up!" she muttered angrily.

Nick's blue gaze lifted to hers. His rough masculine features filled her vision, leaving room for little else. He seemed suddenly too close, his intense eyes reading her much too easily, and alarm made her heart flutter. If only she'd gone to her room and left him alone.

"You don't really think by slamming that album shut you can forget that summer, do you?" Nick sounded amazingly calm as he made the low challenge.

"You have no business snooping among my things," she whispered tautly, replacing the album in the back of the cabinet.

Nick regarded her with lazy indulgence rather than anger. "Triple wanted to show me these albums."

"He doesn't seem to be around at the moment."

Nick shrugged. "I think he got bored. He's playing chess with Sam."

"And you didn't?"

"No. But then I like looking at pictures of you." He lifted a single photograph of her on a Windsurfer and studied it. "You look good in a bikini." The smoldering heat of his eyes engulfed her.

She flushed hotly and tried to grab the snapshot, but he quickly pocketed it next to his heart. His gaze seemed to strip her clothes from her body. Shaken, she dug her fingers tightly into the soft upholstery of the couch.

He was watching her, something flickering in his keen look. "I had forgotten about Lorrie and Jack."

"So had I," she lied warily, still not looking at him.

"You didn't like them dating," Nick persisted.

"Lorrie was so young," Amy replied too quickly. "Besides, she wasn't serious about Jack."

"That was your theory. You thought they were too young for each other. I realized later you were right about that, but she was special to Jack. He never got over her. Sometimes I wonder about Lorrie. She's never married..."

Amy felt sick. "Th-they were a bad combination," she stammered. "Each seemed to bring out the wildness in the other."

"And is that so bad?" Nick queried softly. "That's the way you've always affected me." He smiled at her.

She felt her pulse quicken with unwanted excitement. Her low voice was shaky. "Why must you always turn everything into a seductive remark of some sort?"

"I would think the answer was obvious," he murmured. "Because I want to seduce you. If you'd only let me, maybe I'd stop."

"Thank you, but no thank you," she retorted.

He flashed her one of his charming white grins. "Back to Jack and Lorrie, then."

"I don't want to get back to them."

"But I do." He grinned. "I never felt responsible for my younger brother the way you felt for your sister. Jack always thought he could handle anything that came along."

"So he thought."

"Yes... Maybe I should have done things differently, but I let him live his own life his own way," Nick said gravely. "You never believed Lorrie should do that. You were always in a state of panic that she would get in too deep, that she would get into some relationship she couldn't cope with. She went a little wild there at the end of the summer, but at least now she's all grown up, and you don't have to worry about her anymore."

"Y-yes." Amy gazed out the window, pretending an indifference to the subject she was far from feeling.

Nick swung a lazy glance to her. "Then why are you so upset every time her name is mentioned?"

Her teeth clenched together. "I'm not—upset."

He swore under his breath. "Liar."

He came to her, and she felt his hands grip her bare arms lightly, then more firmly. He turned her around, and his eyes probed into hers. She felt drained.

"If Lorrie's part of what's wrong between us," he said, "Why can't we talk about it? I don't think she liked us dating. She's hardly spoken to me since I came. Don't you think it's time we were honest with each other for a change—about everything?"

Amy felt truly frightened. It was too late for honesty; far too late.

"Do you really think anything you could do or say at this point could make any difference anyway?" she whispered.

"Damn!" His voice was low and angry. Amy always deliberately shut him out. His grip tightened on her arms. When she stiffened from his rough touch, he let her go.

"We are going to talk about it."

"No!"

"Lorrie didn't say something about that last night did she? She didn't twist things around so that you blamed me? She promised me ... *She did say something!* I can see it in your eyes. Surely you don't blame me for what happened?"

He asked these questions so guiltlessly, Amy felt a sickening feeling of nausea. Did he really blame Lorrie for his own weakness of character?

There was nothing she could say. Terror was scrawled across her white face. She stood poised at the doorway to run.

His voice followed after her. "What in the hell are you so afraid of, Amy? The truth isn't something to fear. It's something to face. Run while you can, because that's a liberty I won't allow you much longer. I'm not leaving Los Angeles until I find out what's going on. Six-and-a-half years ago I was too proud to fight for you when you rejected me. I'd never been in love before, never been hurt like that. I couldn't handle it. Not after the way I'd been raised. It was like a repeat of the past when I'd loved my father and mother and they couldn't love me the way I wanted. When you didn't come to Berkeley—when you were so cold over the phone when I asked you why, I thought the hell with her. If she doesn't want me, I don't want her, either. Because I didn't know about Triple, I let you guard your silence. But no more. You spoiled Lorrie. That's part of why she did what she did. She was pretty and pampered, and that's a lethal combination when a girl sets out to seduce a man. Maybe we should confront Lorrie together.''

"No! She's suffered enough at your hands.''

"What the hell's that supposed to mean? I never did a damn thing but try to help her.''

His last words were shouted to an empty room. Amy had run away.

It was four o'clock in the morning. Nick's questions about Lorrie and the past had been so disturbing that Amy hadn't been able to sleep. She had stolen down to the pool to swim.

Moonlight silvered the darkened warm waters of the pool as Amy tossed her filmy cover-up on the tiled floor and stepped into the shallow end. She hadn't turned on the pool lights or the overhead lights because she didn't want anyone to know she was there.

Sparkling waters closed over her. She began to swim an endless number of slow, languid laps, and slowly she felt the tension drain out of her. She finished the last lap in the shallow end.

Amy kept seeing Nick's face. He'd looked so sincere so unafraid, as though he'd had nothing to hide. She kept hearing his words. *The truth isn't something to fear. It's something to face.*

A terrible, unspeakable question had formed in her mind. Perhaps it had always been there, she thought.

Had Lorrie lied in some way about Nick, about everything? The one time Amy had doubted Lorrie's story and had almost gone to Nick, Lorrie had run away and almost died. Her nearly lifeless body had been discovered in the surf. Amy had never dared to question her sister again.

But had she lied?

Lorrie had told little white lies as a child occasionally, lies like the one to Nick about her age all those years ago. But they'd been silly little fibs. Surely she hadn't told a lie about anything so important.

Had she?

Amy felt numb. Cold logic told her she'd never even given Nick a chance to defend himself. Because she'd been so upset, because she'd always protected her sister, Amy had accepted Lorrie's story as gospel.

Stepping out of the pool to retrieve her towel, Amy became aware of a tall, darkened shadow in the doorway.

A scream bubbled from her throat.

"Hush," whispered Nick's raspy voice through the velvet darkness. "There's no reason to be afraid. Not of me."

There was every reason to be afraid.

She wrapped the thick towel around her body protectively. "W-what are you doing here?"

"I thought I heard something, so I came outside to check."

"Well, now that you know who it is, you can leave."

He chuckled. "Now that I know who it is, I'm determined to stay."

"Nick!"

He moved silently toward her. The moonlight made silver ribbons in his golden hair.

"Why won't you go and leave me alone?"

"I've won over everyone but you," he murmured.

"And?"

"It's time I won you," he said softly.

"That's something you'll never do." Amy scampered lightly to the far end of the pool even as he came after her. "I don't want you."

"Yes, you do," he murmured softly, beguilingly. "Tonight I'm going to prove it to you."

"If you dare to force—"

"Oh, I won't need force."

"If you think you can just turn on the charm and have everything your way, you're wrong."

He laughed. "Am I?"

She shrieked at the shock of her wet skin pressed against ice cold glass and steel. She had reached the farthest glass wall, and there was nowhere to run.

His shadow fell across her frightened face, as he caught her wrist and drew her into the hard circle of his arms.

"J-just what do you think you're doing?" she whispered.

"I'm turning on the charm so I can have everything my own way," he murmured huskily. "Thanks for the suggestion."

He brought her close against his body. He was dry and hot, fully clothed; she was wet and warm, and nearly naked.

He held her tightly, not caring that she ruined his silk shirt and wool cashmere slacks. For an instant she was too stunned by the magnitude of what he was doing to react, and then it was too late because she was responding to him as she always had. She felt keenly alive, on the edge of something wonderful and incredibly exciting. She'd been starved so long for the thrill of his lovemaking that she could not resist him.

Tilting her face so that the moonlight fell across it and he could see it properly, he very gently smoothed the damp strands of hair from her eyes. "When I stood there watching you swim, I knew you wanted to be alone. I knew I'd driven you here. I told myself to go, that you didn't want me, that you'd never wanted me." His voice was desperate, agonized. "But I didn't have the strength; I never have where you're concerned. There's never been anyone else for me."

Some part of her wanted to believe him. The past, his betrayal and all the lies and secrets were as nothing. All that mattered was the terrifying emotion in her heart.

She could not stop herself from smiling at him, an achingly sweet smile that must have touched him to the heart because the smile that answered hers was just as sweet in its own masculine way.

"All week I've wondered if you could ever be soft and gentle in my arms again," he murmured. "I'd almost given up hope."

"I'm sorry," she heard the alien, dreamy creature who now possessed her body reply.

Amy stared wordlessly at him as his finger tilted her chin even more, and he bent his golden head to hers and brushed a velvet kiss across her mouth.

The touch of his mouth was heady. She felt dizzy, and her hands slid from his chest to his shoulders to steady herself. The feel of his mouth, firm and hot against hers, the softness of his shirt beneath her fingers, the warmth of his body against her own sent a quiver of bewildering sensation through her.

She drew a quick breath and tentatively dared to kiss him back. Nicholas had already begun to pull away when he felt the faint movement of her lips beneath his. He stood statue-still, his eyes darkening as they met hers. Then something over which he had no control seemed to break inside him, and he crushed her to him fiercely, bending his mouth to hers with more determination than before, his kisses harder this time, and hotter.

His arms tightened around her, drawing her up against himself until they were pressed so closely together that it seemed the flame of his body would burn them into one.

His mouth moved against hers, his tongue moist and seeking as it slid between her parted lips, tasting the molten flesh of her lower lip before nibbling it and sucking it inside his own mouth. Then his tongue slid deeper, and Amy's knees turned to butter as the hot, dark night seemed to revolve around her.

She was drowning; she was dying. And for the first time in years she was really alive.

He was bending her backward, and Amy had to cling tightly to his neck. His tongue touched hers, mated with it, tantalized it. Passionately Amy returned the intimate caress.

Against her flattened breasts she could feel the sudden thunder of his heart. She no longer knew what she did; what he did. She only knew that her tongue was in his mouth, tasting the pleasant warm flavor that was his alone. That his great body was trembling, and suddenly so was hers.

She was hardly conscious of what he did after that, so seduced was she by the ecstasy of sensation his mouth aroused. His hand slid to her breast, shaped it expertly, his fingers brushing against her nipple until it grew rigid. The exquisite pleasure of his touch rippled like hot fluid waves through every part of her.

She stiffened. He was the enemy. Her eyes flashed opened. But was he? Had Lorrie lied? Oh, had she?

Nick kissed Amy again. Whatever he had done, he was her love, and she could not fight him. The same tide of passion sweeping him, swept her.

One taste from the cup of desire and she had to drink more deeply.

Her arms tightened around his neck. Her lashes, fluttered shut, and she was ready to surrender heart and soul to the man she'd despised for more than six years.

When he finally released her, Amy swayed against him. She opened her eyes. Her lips felt moist and swollen from his kisses. Her heart was racing at an unnatural rhythm. She didn't know what to do or say.

Slowly he untied her bikini top, and it fell soundlessly to the tile floor beside her towel.

His dark soft eyes raked her body where her smooth shoulders flowed into lush breasts. "My wife, my darling," he whispered. "You are so beautiful." His hand skimmed lightly over her breasts. Then he caressed her narrow waist and her taut flat belly. His touch was ecstasy. His low voice mesmerized her. "It seems incredible that a body as perfect as yours has ever given birth to a child. To my child."

To Amy the reverently spoken words seemed part of her worst nightmare. Her curved palm flew to her lips, and she gave a little cry of mingled pain and horror. With that single sentence, he broke the spell that had bound her to him, and the past with all its shame and bitterness came back to her.

Though she loved him and he was her husband, he could never be her lover. Never again.

Without bothering to retrieve her towel or the bra of her bikini, she turned and ran.

He was too stunned by her reaction to do anything other than watch her slender form slip away and disappear in the shimmering darkness.

Eight

———

The bedroom door opened, cracking the stillness. Amy leaped to her feet as if she'd been shot.

"Nick?" Her voice was breathy, terrified.

He made no answer. There was only darkness and silence.

She didn't dare make another sound. She had been too upset to think that he might follow her, too upset to remember to lock her door.

Nick paused at the threshold, one large hand on the frame. His gaze was fixed on Amy, his heavy eyes shuttered to conceal their expression.

Amy's breath caught in her throat. Would he be furious or tender? Loving or brutal?

He moved inside and shut the door. She heard the metallic snapping of the bolt as it slid into place. In the darkness he seemed immense.

Amy ran her tongue over her dry lips. She felt the perspiration bead her brow as she shrank back against the bed. Her trembling fingers pulled the warm velvet robe protectively around her naked body.

He came nearer. "Why did you run?" His voice fell softly rather than threateningly, and yet that only made him seem all the more dangerous.

"Because," she gasped. "Oh, Nick. I can't tell you! I—I... I should never have kissed you that way. I should never have led you on."

"But you did."

"I'm sorry."

"I'm not. And this time I'm not going to let you run away."

He strode silently across the room, and pulled her from the bed into his arms. Her wet black hair spilled down the back of her velvet robe, dampening the thick cloth with cold rivulets of water.

"What are you so afraid of?" he demanded.

"I can't tell you—ever."

"Damnation, woman!" he erupted furiously, bitterly, yanking her against his body. "You're enough to try the patience of a saint. And heaven knows, I'm no saint." His fingers dug into her arms, and he shook her until her teeth rattled. "Tell me. Was having my baby alone so awful?"

She merely stared at him helplessly, terrified. His expression seeming to blaze in the darkness, was infinitely tender. Surely no man could look at a woman like that and not be sincere.

"If only you'd told me, I would have been there," he said.

Had Lorrie lied about him? About everything? Oh, had she?

Fear knotted Amy's stomach. Never had she felt more terribly confused. Had she wronged Nick more horribly than any man ever deserved to be wronged?

Deeply ashamed, she began to weep, strong, proud Amy who almost never wept. Oh, if she'd been wrong, she'd never be able to face him.

For an instant he was so stunned he didn't know what to do. At the sight of her tears, the fierce red haze of emotion that had driven him to treat her so brutally died. His breathing slowed and his rough hands gentled.

A terrible guilt assailed him. He had ruined her life by making her pregnant, by forcing her into a marriage she didn't want, by refusing her a divorce. Tonight, he'd used force again. She didn't want him. She never would. He loathed himself for having brought the woman he loved so much pain.

Softly, soothingly, he spoke her name. "There, there, darling. Shh, Amy, sweetheart," he murmured, sliding his fingers through her flowing wet hair, stroking her back.

"Oh, Nick," she whispered, clinging to him tightly, forgetting for the moment her need to fear him. "If only I could have found the strength to stop loving you. If only... Why did you have to come back?"

He hesitated, staring down at her in wonder, only half believing what he heard. *Loving*... She had said she loved him.

After an endless moment she felt his lips on her eyes, kissing away her tears, and slowly her sobs subsided until she rested quietly against him.

As she calmed, he grew aware of her body against his. Her robe had come loose, and only his clothes lay between his skin and her naked body. He could feel her soft breasts pressed against his shirt. He could feel her nipples tighten. She wanted him as much as he wanted her. He could feel it.

They were alone, together, in her bedroom. A man and a woman, and neither had had a mate for two years.

He still couldn't believe the marvel of what she'd admitted. She didn't hate him as he'd feared in his most agonized moments of doubt. She loved him.

"Whatever I've made you suffer, you have to believe that I came back because I wanted to help you," Nick said. "Triple nearly died, and you were all alone. Can't you see that I'll do everything in my power to help you? Whatever it is that's wrong between us, if you'd only tell me what it is, we could work it out. I shouldn't have blamed Lorrie earlier today. I know things aren't that simple."

"No..." The word was a low choked sob. "The only thing you can do is to leave me alone and accept the fact that we can't have a relationship."

"You can't mean that you still want a divorce?"

"Y-yes."

"Look at me, darling," Nick commanded.

Unhappily she lifted her chin an inch, knowing there was no way she could conceal her love for him. It was still shining in her eyes. Gently his hand turned her face to his. His gaze was deep and dark as he accurately read her desperately vulnerable expression. A triumphant smile parted his lips.

"Even though you love me, you want to end our marriage?" he said, incredulous.

"Y-yes."

"Not until I know why."

With a sob she lowered her head. More than anything she longed to seize Triple and have the three of them run away somewhere where they could start over. But even that wouldn't work. The past would always be there to haunt them, to destroy them. "It's not something I can explain," she said tautly.

"Can't you see that you're asking an awful lot?"

"There's too much against us." Her voice quivered with defeat. "We never had a real marriage anyway. You only married me because of Triple. And I only married you because you forced me to. You threatened that paternity suit. You..."

She could feel his muscles tighten; an icy tension froze her heart.

"I remember everything I did then, and I won't give up now, no matter what you say or do," he said angrily. His fingers dug into her arms again and he yanked her viciously against his body. "Even if you won't fight for us, for our happiness, I will."

"It's no use, Nick. There are too many lies. Too..." She stopped herself.

"What are you talking about?"

She buried her face in his shoulder.

He knew of only one weapon to combat her stubborn resistance, and that weapon was his love. His hand traced the length of her slender throat, turning her face once more toward his. She seemed to stop breathing as his gaze explored the lovely radiance of her frightened face. She had expected some harsh argument from him but instead she felt herself being irresistibly drawn by his tenderness.

She felt the pressure of his hand against the small of her back as he arched her body into his, and she sighed. Very slowly his mouth took hers, kissing her lightly at first.

Hesitantly her arms lifted around his shoulders. She opened her lips and let his tongue inside. She was so scared she was shaking like a frightened animal. He crushed her against his body. She could feel the thunder of his heart, but it was racing no faster than her own. The pressure of his mouth hardened, deepened. Gently he stroked and caressed her, his fingers sliding over her arms, her waist, down her back.

Wildfire raced through her veins. She felt dizzy. It was as though some part of her were dissolving into him. She was quivering, trembling. As her fingers dug into the wavy golden silk that curled against his collar, he dragged his mouth reluctantly from hers.

"I love you," he said. "That's the only reason I married you. Triple was just the excuse I used. I would have done anything to make you mine. My life's been hell because you wouldn't have me."

Amy cried out softly. Then she stared back at him dazedly, feeling aroused, lost, frightened. They had both suffered. She wanted him. Nothing else mattered. Not tonight.

Would she later accuse him of forcing her? he wondered. It didn't matter. Nothing mattered. He had to have her.

He stared at her for a long tense moment. The drowsy look of sensuality on her face aroused him more than anything. Her lush lips were parted and swollen from his kisses. Her bewildered amber eyes glowed with desire. The soft gentleness of surrender was in her features.

He felt her fingers remove his shirt from his waistband and slide erotically across the warm skin of his belly. Her touch left a tingly trail of fire.

His eyes darkened to a stormy blue. There was passion in his tense, brown face.

She smiled that sweet, shy smile that made his insides melt, looking at him through her thick lashes. Her hands made lazy caressing circles on his brown skin.

His whole body trembled at the warmth of her soft, sensual touch. For an instant his intense gaze devoured the loveliness of her. Then something inside him broke. He'd gone too long without a woman. Without *his* woman. He needed Amy. He had to have her, or some vital part of him would perish forever.

"Amy; darling, Amy." Gently he wrapped his arms around her and kissed her sweetly, tenderly.

He felt her fingers loosening the buttons of his shirt, sliding the shirt from his shoulders. His arms encircled her like an iron band and he crushed her against the hot, naked wall of his chest. Then he picked her up and carried her to the bed. Her robe opened and his body pressed into hers.

He kissed her until she could hardly breathe. He gripped her arms so hard they hurt, yet his fierce passion sent tremors through her as his mouth slid from her lips, down her throat against the pointed nipples that budded when his wet tongue touched them.

At last he stopped kissing her and stood up to remove the rest of his clothes. She watched him with tremulous fascination, unable to tear her eyes from those broad shoulders, from the exquisite maleness of him.

Slowly he helped her slip out of her robe. Then he lowered his body once more to hers. Every inch of him, every nerve seemed to touch her, and she was enthralled by a new throbbingly alive awareness of him.

His mouth devoured hers. His lips touched her throat, hot against her flesh. His hands played over her breasts. She excited him, and he had to force himself to go slowly.

Gently he drew her close to his chest and stroked her long flowing hair down over her shoulders. As his caresses grew more intense, her body gradually relaxed against his, and a tiny moan escaped her lips.

When he came into her, gently at first, and then more fiercely, she cried out against his shoulder. He felt her fingernails dig into his skin. Nick forced himself to stop, and he held her closely as he waited for her to grow accustomed to him. He kissed her brow tenderly; then he murmured something low and inaudible against her ear.

He whispered her name. "Amy. Are you all right?"

"Yes." The single word was a throb of desire that quickened his own savage longing. For years he'd lived without her, without this, without any woman, because he wanted no woman but her, and now she was his. As she pressed her hands into the small of his back and drew him closer, he made a silent vow to himself that he'd never lose her again.

Stirred past reason by her acceptance of him, he could restrain himself no longer. He began to move again, driving into her with a wild, urgent force. An answering excitement rose within her, mounting higher and higher as he sought to please her. Her lips half opened, and her teeth came together in a strange agony of delight as a dazzling tide of emotion flamed through her. She clung to him desperately.

He was hot, and she was hot. It was as if their love were a flame and they were consumed by it.

Giving a short, hoarse cry, he thrust inside her one last time, ending the deep hard rhythm, holding her tightly to his body. She clung to him, almost unconscious in her own pleasure as violent sensations exploded in every soft tissue of her being.

For one keen, exhilarating moment they were one.

As she held on to him fiercely, a joy Nick had never known before pierced him. Amy had gone wild in his arms.

Then it was over, and the glorious moment slipped away, dissolving too quickly into a hazy, warm memory of desire. His body loosened its clasp on hers.

She slid to the other side of the bed, silently rolling over and turning her back to him. He heard her as she began to sob quietly in the darkness, and all the ecstasy he'd known only a minute before drained from his heart.

His loving her had changed nothing.

Amy awoke to the startling image of Nick's golden head
bathed in glorious sunlight, but she did not at first compre-
hend that there was anything abnormal about waking in his
arms. The room was warm, the cotton sheets soft against
her body, and she felt enveloped in a cocoon of sated sensuality.

Her raven hair flowed over his arms like glistening skeins
of spilled silk. His body heat had been like a magnet in the
night, drawing her close, and at some point she had snug-
gled against his shoulder.

Slowly it came to her that although it was delicious lying
with him, it was something she should never have done.
Amy swallowed hard and averted her eyes from Nick.

She was naked, her arms and legs tangled intimately in
his. One of his thighs was sprawled across her stomach,
locking her tightly beneath him. His fingers were curved
possessively over her breast. Her freshly awakened body felt
throbbingly aware of him.

As she remembered what she had done, remorse washed
over her. At the same time she felt every flutter and subtle
nuance of sensation at his slightest movement.

Why? Why had she let it happen?

How could she have stopped it?

Hadn't she known that from the moment he'd returned,
such a night as the one they'd shared was inevitable?

Trying not to awaken him, she made an attempt to shift
out of his embrace, but that was not possible. He had only
been pretending to sleep. He caught her playfully by the
wrist and pulled her back.

"Good morning," his sleepy voice rasped lovingly.

His thigh was rock hard against her hip bone. His fingers were tongues of flame upon her slender wrist as he drew her nearer.

As Nick's indolent gaze swept the length of her womanly form, the warm tremor of desire made his eyes light hotly.

Her eyes met his, and she saw at once that it would never be possible to convince him that what had happened had been no more than an irresistible moment of madness, that it must never, never happen again. His eyes staked his claim to a fresh and torrid passion.

His mouth lowered to hers, and he kissed her with such bewildering tenderness, that all her thoughts of protest died. Hands that might have fought to push him away, trembled and then slid around his neck and clasped him passionately. A low moan escaped her lips.

He kissed her lips, her throat, her breasts, his mouth moving ever lower, stirring her, awakening in her the old aching need.

How could it seem like forever since she'd been loved when it had only been a few short hours?

With his mouth he worshiped her, and soon nothing mattered but his lips and the flame of desire flaring in the center of her being.

His golden head nestled into her belly. Gently he forced her thighs apart. She felt the roughness of his cheeks as they slid rhythmically against her velvet skin. He drove her wild.

Her body writhed shamelessly. Her fingers curled into the golden thickness of his hair and pulled him even closer until she felt the building of an elemental and primitive explosion from deep within her being.

"Nick." His name was a raw agonized sound.

Dear Lord! How she loved him! She was frantic for him. Her cry rent the air as rapture flooded every living cell of her body.

Afterward they lay quietly for a long time. She was ashamed of how completely she had surrendered herself to him, of how deeply she adored him.

Vaguely she wondered how she would ever find the strength to fight the battle that lay before her.

It was Nick who got out of bed first. "I'd forgotten how hot-blooded you are," he said on a low, self-satisfied chuckle. He grabbed her hand and pulled her up.

"I had forgotten, too," she admitted, unable to deny his power.

It was something she had struggled to forget.

"Next time," he whispered, "it will be your turn to make love to me."

His eyes were brilliant, and the answering excitement his words aroused filled her with dread. There couldn't be a next time. There mustn't be...

But even as she thought of how she must deny him, she turned her lips to his and let him claim them in a passionate kiss.

She loved him, no matter what he'd done. But if she had been misled all those years ago, if it was *she* who had wronged *him*, would his love for her be as strong?

When Nick and Amy came into the kitchen, they were astonished to find Sam and Triple already there, having waited for them before eating breakfast. A mood of celebration hung in the air. Sam usually didn't cook, but he was up and about, whistling and smiling by the stove, his cane forgotten against the wall.

On the counter was a generous platter of fried ham and eggs, English muffins, and glasses of fresh orange juice. A radiant Triple was rushing around the kitchen, carrying plates and silverware, and setting the table, showing an unusual amount of exuberance for a task he normally found tedious. Only Lorrie was absent.

The minute Nick and Amy stepped inside, an embarrassed hush fell, then Sam boisterously greeted them. "Great morning!"

"Couldn't be better," Nick replied on a bold vibrant note, smiling broadly as he encircled a glowing Amy with his arms and drew her close. Triple watched with shining eyes as his father tenderly kissed his blushing mother on the forehead. Nick's lovingly reverent expression was such that no one but a blind person could have mistaken the change in their relationship since the night before. If Nick had shouted it from the rooftops, he could not have gotten his message across more clearly.

As Triple danced across the kitchen to get the paper napkins and set them out, the boy began to sing to himself in that raucous off-key way that so reminded Amy of Nick. Suddenly Triple gave a cry of joy and threw himself into his parents' arms. "Are we a real family now? Is Dad going to stay for good?"

Amy could only clutch her child tightly with shaking fingers. She heard Nick's voice, deep and gentle, filled with love.

"Yes, I'll be staying—for good."

"Is he, Mom? I mean—really?"

She felt Nick's arms around her. She looked down at Triple. She wanted it to be true so much that she could not deny it.

"Really, son," Nick said softly.

"Breakfast's ready!" Sam said.

"Sit down everyone," Nick murmured. He sat at the head of the table and began shoveling eggs and ham and a muffin onto everybody's plates.

Amy couldn't look at him. Her eyes were swimming with tears of happiness. A fragile hope was beginning to take root in her heart.

Nick began to make plans. "Of course, this means I'll have to make some changes, but I've already spoken to Sebastian about moving the headquarters of South Sails to L.A., and he has no objections."

"You were that sure?" Amy whispered, looking at Nick wonderingly from across the table.

He merely smiled at her boldly in that confident way of his. "After breakfast, I'm going to call my father and Mercedes. I want them to come immediately. And maybe I'll even invite Jeb," he said smiling ruefully.

Jeb was Nick's older half brother, and there had always been a friendly rivalry between them, instead of the closeness that had existed between Nick and Jack.

"Oh boy! Grandfather and Mercedes and Uncle Jeb are coming!"

Triple knew his father's relatives because every July Nick had dutifully flown his son to Texas to their ranch for a week.

"Why don't we go to the ranch and see them, Dad! Mercedes wrote me at Christmas that she'd bought a pony named Nugget. He's small enough for me to ride. She said he's as sweet and gentle as a puppy and comes up to you to be petted. She said Nugget can talk and Nugget wants me to come because there's nobody there little enough to ride him. He gets lonely for a kid to play with."

"Soon," Nick said, grinning. "First you have to get well and catch up on your schoolwork."

Amy said, "Nick, don't you think, maybe...you're rushing things? Maybe we should get used to one another..."

"I'm not rushing things. We've been married five years, and you've never met my family. We have the rest of our lives to get used to one another."

"You'll like them, Mom!"

Nick and Sam and Triple kept talking enthusiastically of all the things they would do as a family. Amy toyed with her food, twisting her fork in her egg as she listened to them. She felt weighed down by doubt. Nevertheless, she wanted to believe what they all believed—that she and Nick could really become a normal married couple with in-laws and family breakfasts like this one, that the past and a long-ago lie would not tear up all their lives again.

She had been alone too long. She wanted to be happy, but before that was possible, she had to see Lorrie.

Nick called his family in Texas. Later he went out to see Sebastian to arrange the South Sails move. It was with some difficulty that Amy convinced Triple he had to go back to his bed and rest. He agreed when she allowed him to take two jars filled with spiders and his chrysalis to bed. Only after Nick had gone and Triple was settled, did Amy dare to call Lorrie.

Lorrie's voice was immediately defensive and so faint Amy could hardly hear it. "He told you something, didn't he? That's why you called."

Amy's hands felt clammy. Had Lorrie really lied? Amy almost blurted the question before she realized she had to proceed cautiously. "We've got to talk."

"I don't want to see...*him*," Lorrie continued in the same fearful defensive tone.

Amy had to steel herself. "He'll be out all day."

"I don't want—"

"If I have to, I'll come over there." Amy had never spoken to her sister so firmly.

"A-Amy—"

"It's time we faced the truth. I have to know...
everything. I want you to come to the house and talk to
me."

Lorrie only made a strangled, guttural sound.

Their phone call had been over for an hour before Lorrie
came. Amy had paced the floor impatiently, wondering as
the hour grew later, if Lorrie's faint courage had failed her.
Then Amy heard her sister outside.

Amy threw open the door. The day was full of brilliant
sunshine. Lorrie stood on tiptoe as if poised for flight. She
was standing in the shadows, her face white with panic.

"Oh, Lorrie." Amy hugged her gently. "There's no reason for you to be afraid—not of me."

At her kindness, Lorrie seemed to shrink even more
deeply into the shadows.

A telling glance passed between the two sisters before
Lorrie allowed herself to be led wordlessly inside. Amy's
face was flushed and radiant. Lorrie looked pale and
haunted.

Amy fought to ignore the twist of guilt brought by the
knowledge that she was the cause of her sister's anguish.

"You look different," Lorrie said in a trembling voice,
taking in Amy's brilliant eyes and her glowing expression.
"It's *him*."

Amy could not deny it. She whispered breathlessly,
"Yes."

When Amy closed the door to the den so that they could
be alone, she didn't notice that the door didn't quite latch,
that it fell back from the jamb an inch or so.

"I-it's the way you were before," Lorrie stammered hesitantly, not quite daring to look at Amy, "that summer...
when you were planning to go away with him."

"I love him."

Lorrie's eyes were immense. "But..." She was trembling as though on the verge of hysteria.

Amy saw the agony in her sister's eyes, and it was all she could do to quell the powerful maternal feelings that swelled in her heart. She had always taken care of Lorrie and had never willfully caused her pain. "I don't care what he did. He wants to put the past behind us."

"You really love him...more..."

"More than anything. I can't deny it any longer, even though I know it brings you pain. That doesn't mean I don't love you, Lorrie. Or Triple. It's just that Nick's first. Even after...what happened. I have to know about that night...when you were together. Yesterday he tried to talk to me about it, but I wouldn't let him. He seemed so honest, so forthright, and because of our lie to him, I couldn't talk to him."

Lorrie began to shiver. She looked like a worried child who knew she'd done wrong and was afraid of being punished.

"I wanted to talk to you first—alone," Amy said. "I want a real marriage with him. That's why we—all of us—have to face the whole truth about that night. You want me to be happy, don't you?"

Lorrie's fearful eyes had grown even larger, and she looked more deeply troubled and uncertain than ever. "I— I want you to be happy," Lorrie began slowly, "and I've known you weren't—not for a long time. It's all my fault, too. But I've never known what to do about it. I'm not brave like you. I've always been such a ninny."

Amy took Lorrie's cold hands in hers and kissed them. "I don't blame you."

Lorrie's face was taut and drawn as she regarded Amy closely. "But what about Triple?" Lorrie whispered. "What about him?"

"I said we have to tell Nick the whole truth."

"You can't mean—"

There was a gulf of silence. Amy's face grew as ashen and doubt-filled as Lorrie's.

"We have to tell him that you're really Triple's natural mother, Lorrie."

The silence between them deepened as Lorrie stared at her in mute horror.

Neither spoke. Neither moved. It was as if a freezing fear held them both in its paralyzing grip.

"You know we do!" Amy said.

Lorrie pulled her hands free. "But you promised we'd never," she shouted, "that no one would ever know that you weren't his real mother."

Amy went on talking. "We have to tell him that when we found out you were pregnant with his child, you wouldn't let me go to him. So I went to Sebastian instead and said I was in trouble. We went away together. You pretended to be me. You used my identification. You dyed your hair black. We have to tell him everything, every single detail." Amy swallowed back the lump in her throat. "How difficult the birth was; how the doctor said you should never have another child."

"No..." Lorrie turned away. "We can't. We just can't.

"Nick has to know. We can't make a true, fresh start unless we deal with this honestly."

Lorrie was standing at the window. She turned. Her white face was drawn with horror.

"We can't ever do that! Don't you see? We can't ever!" Tears were streaming down her face.

"Why not?"

"Because you'll lose both Triple and Nick for sure, if you do."

"That's a risk I have to take."

"You still don't get it, do you?"

"Get what?" Amy whispered, dreading the answer, wondering, doubting, half hoping.

"There's something you don't know. Something I never told you. Something so awful that you'll hate me forever when I tell you. I only did it because..." Lorrie wrung her hands. Her eyes pleaded for an understanding Amy couldn't give her.

A terrible knot began to form in Amy's stomach. She felt queasy with fear. "What are you saying?"

Lorrie's eyes fell guiltily. "Nick didn't sleep with me! It was Jack! Not Nick! Nick came home and found us together. He sent Jack away. Nick stayed and talked to me. He told me Jack and I were too young for that sort of relationship, that we weren't old enough to accept the responsibilities that went along with it. He told me how worried you were about me—that I was to tell you everything. I looked up and saw you. He told me he loved you, that he was going to marry you, that someday when I was older I would find a man who would love me in the same way. When you ran away, I began to see a way."

"No..." For a moment Amy stood petrified, her face as bloodless as if she were a statue cut from some pale, cold slab of marble.

"I know it was wrong, what I did, to sleep with Jack, to lie," Lorrie said quietly. "I've known it for years, but I didn't know how to make it right again. Maybe I didn't want to make it right. I've never had your ability to fight...for anything. I was sixteen. I was jealous and scared of Nick. All I knew was that he was going to take you away. I'd lost Mother. Daddy was never there for me. You were all I had. You were like my mother, only sweeter. You always put me first, spoiled me. I couldn't lose you, Amy. Oh, I was wrong. I loved you so much, but I ruined your life. There've been times I've come close to telling you, but I never could. I thought I was doing the right thing. I thought you'd forget him. Maybe I would have told you the truth, but then I got pregnant. I let you assume Nick was the father, and the lie went on and on. I was too young to be a mother. I couldn't face bringing up a baby. You said we had to tell Nick the truth because it was his child, and I got so scared I ran away."

"N-no..."

"I wanted to die that night. I walked along those slippery rocks and fell into the ocean. I wanted to die like Mother, but I didn't. You were so scared for me, so sweet to me, and I made you promise you wouldn't ever go to Nick. So you went to Sebastian. Then Nick found out, and forced you to marry him. Everything got so twisted and mixed up, and I just couldn't see any way we'd ever straighten it out. But don't you see, you can't tell Nick the truth. Not now. He's not Triple's father at all. He'll only hate us both."

Amy studied her sister, seeing her fragile, childlike face and yet not seeing it, realizing for the first time in a kind of dazed amazement that she had lived with Lorrie for years and had never known her true character.

Oh, the terrible, terrible weapons of the weak.

"Say something, Amy, p-please... Forgive..."

Amy kept looking at her sister, whose tear-filled eyes were downcast, whose bright head dropped disconsolately with shame.

A tight band closed around Amy's heart. She could hardly breathe.

Sickened with a mixture of remorse, disgust, and shame, she whirled away and said nothing.

What was there she could say? Lorrie wasn't a little girl anymore, though she still acted like one far too often. This wasn't a childish bit of mischief that could be instantly forgiven or forgotten. Amy saw how wrong she had been to spoil her. How wrong...

Nick was innocent. He'd never been unfaithful to her. Amy had believed Lorrie. Amy's heart felt near bursting with the pain of it all. Oh, why had she? Was it just that she was used to always believing her younger sister, to always protecting her? That was no excuse. Amy had hardened her heart with hatred toward an innocent man, a man who'd loved her. She'd had so little faith in herself, so little faith in him, she'd never given him a chance to defend himself. She'd been so selfish and blind with her own hurt that she'd built up a case against him to soothe her wounds. She'd posed as the mother of his child, accepting money from Sebastian, accepting marriage from Nick, and everything she'd done was based on a horrendous lie. She'd lived on hate. She treated him cruelly, deliberately keeping him from Triple. She'd thought he'd destroyed all their lives, but he hadn't. She had.

He would never forgive her.

She would never be able to forgive herself.

Through the haze of her pain, Amy heard Lorrie's voice. It was indistinct, blurred, but Amy caught every word.

"Don't you see? You can't tell him. You've been unhappy for so long. You deserve happiness. Don't tell him, and everything will be all right."

That was the same destructive pattern of thinking that had gotten them all into such trouble.

A dull hammer pounded in Amy's temple. Nothing would ever be all right again.

If she didn't tell the truth, she would hate herself forever.

If she told the truth, she would lose Nick forever.

A lonely, black despair closed over her.

She wasn't even aware that Lorrie had slipped quietly out of the house.

Nine

The afternoon sun cast filaments of fire upon the glimmering waves. Purple shadows slanted across the beach.

Amy sat motionless in the brooding silence of her bedroom and waited for Nick to come home. She had to tell him everything—as soon as possible.

But how was she ever going to convince him that she had believed she was doing right by going to Sebastian and telling him *she* was pregnant? Amy had been used to shouldering responsibility, to fighting her sister's battles. Besides, from the day Amy had first lifted Triple into her arms in the hospital, she'd wanted him to be her child more than anything. From that first moment, when his tiny hand had curled around her little finger and clung, she'd been his mother. Everything else had seemed insignificant. The shame of letting everyone believe her an unwed mother had seemed as nothing when compared to the prospect of putting him up for adoption. She'd loved him with all the fierce, protective loyalty only a mother could feel.

Amy had married Nick when he'd threatened a custody battle, only because she'd been afraid that he might somehow find out the truth about Triple's parentage. If Nick had found out then that she wasn't Triple's natural mother, she thought he might have taken the child away form her.

She'd misjudged Nick. She only hoped there was some way to make up for it.

An eternity later the front door banged open, and she heard Nick's heavy tread in the hall. Her heart lurched as his footsteps approached her bedroom. Then he paused, and the house became silent. What was he doing?

The minutes ticked by, one by one, and he didn't come. Where was he? What was he doing? She twisted her hands. Then she leaped to her feet. She would rather face being drawn and quartered than tell the man she loved what she'd done, but she had to get it over with. She left her room and went downstairs.

Standing outside the den, Amy heard the whisper of excited male voices. Silently she opened the door a crack and peered in. Nick and Sam were sitting on the couch, huddled over a new computer chess board resting on a low table. Nick's raspy voice was a murmur of patient explanation.

Her heart contracted in fresh shame as she watched this latest example of Nick's kindness. He was very busy with the South Sails move, but he had taken the time to buy her father a gift.

"I need to talk to you, Nick," she said so quietly her words didn't quite carry across the room.

He glanced up quizzically. A glare of copper-gold light flooded into the room. Her hair was tumbling about her shoulders in fire-tipped waves, her bosom heaving nervously. He flashed her a dazzling smile.

"Come here, darling," he said, "and see what I found for Sam."

As he continued to look at her steadily, she felt the warm glow of his love, and her hand fluttered to her heart with new misgivings.

"I—I was worried—you were gone so long," she murmured, too ashamed to say more.

"I had to look in several stores to find this," he said, pulling her down beside him. Tenderly his lips grazed her icy brow. "I was just telling Sam that Mercedes, Dad and Jeb are coming tomorrow."

"Tomorrow..." The word died halfway up her throat.

Misinterpreting her anguished tone to be lack of enthusiasm at the prospect of his parents' imminent visit, Nick folded her freezing cold hands in his. "I know there's not much time for you to get ready, darling, but Apolonia's better now. And we'll do a lot of eating out. I'll pitch in. I tried to find Triple to tell him, but I couldn't find him anywhere. His room was as silent as a tomb and as tidily arranged as a museum. It's obvious he hasn't been near it in hours. His twelve-meter is lying on its side by the pool."

"It's always a bad sign when Triple doesn't mess up his room or when he gets quiet and goes off by himself," Amy said.

Normally Amy would have been more worried about Triple's odd disappearance, but she was too preoccupied with her own problem to give it the attention it deserved.

She turned away from Nick and her father, from the dancing red lights of the computer board as they moved the chess pieces. There was no way she could spoil Nick's family's visit by telling him the truth now. She would have to wait.

Triple's behavior remained strange even after Jeb, Mercedes and Wayne Jackson arrived. Though they brought Triple presents and made a fuss over him, he kept to his room as much as possible. In the past when Triple had a quiet period, it had usually been a lull before the storm.

Amy immediately loved Nick's family, and because she did, her problem was magnified. It was as if her secret were growing to affect them.

Wayne Jackson was an older, almost exact replica of Nick. He had Nick's same restless, excessive energy, his indomitable will, the same pale hair—silvered now—and brilliant blue eyes. Wayne was larger than life, stomping around Malibu in his jeans, custom-made boots and Stetson. He was a Texan to the core, outgoing and friendly to a fault, stopping strangers on the beach with a howdy and a smile, and treating them to long, drawn-out conversation, Texas-style. At first they would stare at him in wonder and listen with more wonder, privacy being the most highly prized of all Malibu commodities. But soon he had them up at the house for a drink, introducing Amy to neighbors she'd lived near for years and never met.

Mercedes was quieter, darker and lovely, even though she was almost sixty. She had the slender, graceful figure of a girl, and a beautiful way of moving. She had formerly been Mercedes Montez, the great Mexican ballerina, before giving up her career to marry Wayne. Her long, black hair was streaked with ribbons of silver. She was not so blatantly a Texan as Wayne and Jeb. She was more sophisticated, having lived all over the world. Mercedes had a melodious Spanish accent, rather than a flat Texas drawl, but for all her outward softness and femininity, Amy sensed in her a formidable will the equal of her husband's.

Jeb was dark and quiet, more like his mother than his father; yet he was a mixture of both these strong personalities. He was tall and bold, heavily muscled and strong. He exuded an aura of command and managed an empire bigger than many countries. In some indefinable way he reminded her of Nick. There was a restlessness in Jeb. It seemed as if he were in conflict with himself, as if despite everything he had, there was something missing in his life. Amy sensed a deep affection between the two brothers, yet she was immediately aware of their rivalry.

"Amy's too pretty and smart to be your wife," Jeb had drawled lazily on first meeting her, pulling her into his arms before he tipped his hat back and kissed her. "No wonder you haven't brought her to Texas to meet your big brother."

"That wasn't why."

A look flashed between the brothers.

"Easy, boy," Jeb said, letting her go. "Just welcoming her into the family Texas-style."

Amy found herself in the possessive iron grip of her husband's arms.

"Maybe it's time you got married again," Nick said.

Jeb's warm, black eyes lingered on Amy. "Maybe so. You've certainly proved that finding the right wife could be a worthwhile enterprise."

Nick was careful not to leave Amy and Jeb alone together for long.

Amy wasn't able to resist teasing Nick.

"Surely you trust your own brother."

"Of course, I trust him. About as far as I can throw him."

"Nick..."

"Jeb's the oldest Jackson son. He thinks he's a king. He rules a world. He has to know he's not a king here. Not in my house."

"He's your brother."

"My half brother. A legitimate son. Neither of us has ever been able to forget that."

"You love him?"

"That goes without saying. But love doesn't have to blind you to the defects in someone's character. He used to resent me when I was a kid, when I came to Texas—and I resented him. I thought he had everything—a father and mother who loved and wanted him, the ranch. He could do everything better than me. There's nobody that knows more about horses, cows and oil than Jeb. He belonged in the family. I didn't. But I've carved out a life of my own. You're mine, not his. He can have the ranch. He can have everything else. All I want is you."

Nick had made love to her so passionately that night that Amy had almost been glad of his jealousy.

Mercedes was a natural matchmaker. She was obviously thrilled to find Nick so happy. Once when the men had gone out with Sebastian to sail on Sebastian's *Marauder*, taking Triple with them, Mercedes caught Amy alone.

Apolonia was busy as usual in the garden, so they made tea themselves and carried their cups down to the pergola where they could watch the water and the glamorous people meandering along the beach, waving effusively to one another but rarely speaking. Mercedes and Amy talked of general things for a while, joking that dinner might be late if Apolonia didn't abandon her gardening for the kitchen. At last a comfortable silence fell between them.

"This may be my only chance to talk to you privately," Mercedes said gently. "I wanted to say that I'm happy you and Nick are together at last. I knew, of course, about your marriage, your separation. When there was no divorce, I could not help hoping there wouldn't ever be one."

There was such a motherly warmth about Mercedes that Amy did not mind the personal turn of the conversation.

"We still have problems," Amy said, biting her bottom lip. "I'm not sure we can work them out."

"You will," Mercedes said softly. "I can tell by the way you look at each other. Sometimes it takes a while." She hesitated. "Wayne and I were separated once. I'm sure Nick told you. We nearly lost each other because of a terrible misunderstanding. It was all my fault, but of course, I didn't see it that way at the time. Injured feelings have a way of blinding one to the truth. Wayne even turned to another woman during that time, and the result was Nick. When I learned that I had been wrong about Wayne, I had to swallow my pride and go to him and beg his forgiveness. Neither of us knew about Nick for a long time."

"And Wayne forgave you?"

"Not immediately. It took time. The first months of a reconciliation are the most difficult. Sometimes it isn't easy for two people to find each other no matter how much they want to. And when we found out about Nick, it wasn't long before I was even glad about him. Do you know that he's more like Wayne than any of my other three sons were? I have come to love him so much, sometimes I have to remind myself he's not my son. One need not give birth to a child to feel like his mother. Nick has been alone too long. Make him happy, my dear. You have your child. It's too bad you had to come so close to losing Triple before Nick and you could find each other again."

"Triple was very sick. I was so frightened until Nick came. He's been . . . wonderful."

"Sometimes it takes a crisis to help us put life into perspective." Mercedes's eyes were moist. "I know all about the fear of losing a child. Such an experience has a powerful effect. I've lost two, you know."

"Of course, I knew about Jack."

"Years ago, I lost my only little girl, Julia. We never found her..."

"Nick never told me."

"It's not something any of us have spoken of, but I've never forgotten her. I've always wondered if she was dead or alive."

"That must be dreadful."

"When you're as old as I, you will know that life is filled with both sorrow and happiness. Without the one, you cannot appreciate the other. The tragedies brought me closer to my husband and the children I have left. I have much to be thankful for. So do you. Make Nick happy."

If only it were that simple, Amy thought.

The Jacksons' presence in their lives increased Amy's awareness of how wonderful being truly married to Nick could be—if only she was not constantly haunted by the guilt of her secret. It ate at her heart, robbing her of genuine happiness. The Jacksons liked her and trusted her, and sometimes a pressure built in her to shout that nothing was the way they thought it was. But she kept her silence.

To entertain the Jacksons, they went sailing, dined in the best restaurants so that Mercedes could stargaze, and went sight-seeing. Jeb and Wayne proved to be as reckless behind the wheel of a car as Nick was. From time to time when they didn't know she was listening, she would hear them singing in the same raucous off-key manner Nick had when he was alone. Even if Nick had been born a bastard, he was one of them.

Mercedes told Triple she'd brought him an autographed picture of Nugget, the little horse she'd bought for him.

"Horses can't write," Triple had said.

"Nugget is a very special pony." Mercedes turned the picture over. "He writes in his own way." On the photograph's back was a hoofprint.

Triple burst into laughter. "I have to come to Texas, soon."

It was a whirlwind, fun-filled visit. Triple remained quiet, which was fortunate in a way because he was on his best behavior. Nick was a marvelous host. He told Amy that soon he would take her to Australia to meet Tad, his other brother, who ran the Australian cattle stations that belonged to the Jackson Ranch.

Triple kept asking about the Jackson jet. Saturday afternoon Wayne and Jeb took Triple and Amy to the airport to meet their pilot who was a beautiful redhead named Megan MacKay. She'd grown up on the Jackson Ranch. Megan took Triple aboard and gave him a tour of the jet. For the first time Triple was his old energetic self, and Amy knew he would soon make a complete recovery.

Triple took great interest in examining everything. There was a lot of excitement for a while when he got lost somewhere at the airport. Then he popped up. He seemed quite pleased when he came home that evening, and he did not go to his room until he was made to.

On Sunday it was time for the Jacksons to leave. Amy and Nick drove them to the airport to see them off. Because it was late and Triple said he wasn't feeling well and wanted to go to bed, Amy and Nick had gone to the airport alone.

When they returned they were happy, but a little sad, too, because the Jacksons were gone. Amy was exhausted, both emotionally and physically from their visit.

Nick and Amy were in their bedroom undressing for bed, and as Amy stared at her impassive pale face in the mirror she made a silent vow. "Tomorrow... Tomorrow when I'm rested, I'll tell him everything."

Nick came up from behind her, and his golden head bent over her dark one. "My family loves you," he said huskily. "Just as I do."

"And I love them."

"I think we have the beginnings of a real marriage."

She turned away and bit her bottom lip.

"More than the beginnings," he went on in the same velvet tone. "Have you ever asked yourself what has held us together for all these years, even when we almost never saw each other? Was it only our child? Or was there something more, some deeper reason why neither of us took the steps to end our relationship?"

She was silent. Her heart hammered against her rib cage. She could not say anything. If he knew the truth—

"I want another child," he said.

"You keep rushing me."

He came close to her again. She had taken off everything but her silk slip. His hands glided slowly over her spine to press her against his hard lithe body. His voice was soft against her ear, his mouth brushing the bottom edge of her earlobe. "Because I love you. Because I sense that even now you're not completely mine. There are still some barriers between us. If we had another child and could share everything about the experience..."

Her head was spinning as he kissed the back of her neck. "N-no. That's not the answer."

"This time it will be different," he murmured. "I'll be there with you. I've always wondered what you went through having Triple."

He was turning her. His mouth followed the wildly pulsing vein in her neck to the sensitive hollow of her throat.

"Nick..."

He let her go.

His expression was grave as he studied her. "You've never talked about it. Was it a difficult birth?" He misunderstood the silent agony in her eyes, and his demand became more passionate. "Tell me. I have to know."

"Y-yes. It was difficult." That wasn't exactly a lie, but it wasn't the whole truth, either. Dear God! She had to do better than that. "Nick, tomorrow...we'll talk. I'll tell you everything," she said desperately.

Oh, what would he think of her when he found it was Lorrie's pregnancy, not hers he would be hearing about? After Lorrie had nearly drowned, her pregnancy had been difficult. The baby had come early. Lorrie had been terrified, childlike, so hysterical the nurses had let Amy stay with her. Amy could still remember Lorrie's piercing screams. They had torn her heart out.

Nick was watching Amy, reading the emotions on her face. Then his arms wrapped around her. She breathed in the intoxicating smell of him. He crushed her face against his so that the moist softness of her cheek scraped the rough stubble of his beard. "It always upsets me when I think of you facing all of that alone. Never again, my love. I will always be with you. You must believe that."

Suddenly she was sobbing.

"Why are you crying?"

"B-because I love you so much, and I'm so afraid of losing you."

"You'll never lose me."

He crushed her lips beneath his mouth, devouring them in a rapturous assault of passion that left her breathless and dazed.

He kissed her again and again. Deftly his hands slid the straps of her slip down her bare arms so that the flimsy silk fell to her waist. He cupped her breasts lovingly.

She was hardly conscious of what he did after that. Desire flooded her mind and body, sweeping her away on a dizzying tide of emotion. Amy forgot the monumental lie that stood between them. She wanted the oblivion of forgetfulness.

As he drew her down upon the bed, she forgot everything but his dominating kisses and the fierce, keen urgency to belong to him.

Nick fell asleep at once, but she couldn't. As the warmth of her passion ebbed, the old icy fear stole over her heart. Amy knew what Lorrie must have felt through the years. She was beginning to realize that if she didn't tell Nick the truth, the misery would never stop. It would always be there, twisting everything, marring with guilt even the happiest moments of their marriage.

She got up, pulled on her robe, and went out onto the balcony. Tomorrow... How would she ever find the strength to tell him? How could she face the risk of losing him? Where would she start?

Nick, there's a little matter we have to talk about. It's nothing really. It's just that I'm not really Triple's mother. She imagined his look of blank shock. *And that's not all. You're not his father, either. You never should have married me...*

Dear Lord, she thought. How unbearable it would be to watch Nick's love turn to hate.

She looked out to sea, then across the length of the shadowed balcony, as if somehow she would find the answers she sought from that still, black infinity.

It was then that she noticed Triple's open door. Slowly it dawned on her that something was wrong.

She rushed across the balcony to his room, remembering how he had said he wasn't feeling well enough to go to the airport, how he'd insisted on going to bed before it was even dark, before they'd left for the airport. Even though he'd kept to his room more than usual lately, that had been a first. Recuperating or not, Triple had never once in his brief, active life volunteered to go to bed early.

Amy stepped into his room and for an instant felt immediate relief when she saw her little boy's form nestled peacefully beneath his covers.

The room was ice-cold. She went to him. No one could sleep in such a room. Unless... Fear gripped her heart.

He was so still, so soundless.

No... Triple had to be all right!

As she bent down to touch him, she saw that the figure in the bed had the gigantic head of a stuffed gorilla.

She screamed. Then she flipped on the light and yanked back the bedspread.

There was nothing but a carefully arranged mound of pillows and stuffed animals.

Triple was gone.

She was almost relieved.

Even as she stared at the empty bed, she saw the note on the bedside table. Triple never wrote anything unless he had something important to say.

She picked up the note. It was horribly misspelled, but it's meaning was all too clear. *Yuore not my parnets! You dnot love me!*

It could mean only one thing. Triple had found out the truth somehow.

She should have told Nick. Oh, why hadn't she?

The note fell through her stiff fingers as Nick rushed into the room.

"I heard your scream. Where's..."

She shuddered at the dark grimness of his features. "Gone..." Her voice trailed away. "He left... this."

She picked up the note and handed it to him.

"This doesn't explain anything! What the hell's going on? If you know something, tell me."

She felt tense, afraid to speak, afraid not to. She stared at him, drinking in the carved glory of his male face, realizing in that moment how very much she had always loved him. She was so terribly close to losing him. "Oh, Nick," she sobbed helplessly.

Instantly he pulled her into his arms. "We're in this together, darling. We'll find him. It isn't as if this is the first time he's pulled something like this."

With a gasping cry of pain, she pushed him away. Bitter tears filled her eyes. She felt his strong arms try to pull her back against his chest. Even though she longed for the heat of his body to warm her, she pivoted and turned away. She was glad her back was to him, and he couldn't see the agony and pain in her eyes. "I don't deserve your love."

Again he tried to draw her into his arms and she wouldn't let him. He looked hurt, baffled. He couldn't know it wasn't his touch she feared, but his anger.

"Triple's run away, and it's my fault," she said. "Nick, I've kept a terrible secret from you, and somehow Triple found out. He's so little. He can't understand. If anything happens to him, I'll never forgive myself. You should have divorced me when you had the chance."

"So we're back to that. The first crisis, and it's, good-bye, Nick." His face hardened. "I told you I'd give you a divorce only when you told me the truth."

"I don't know where to begin."

"Damn it!" Anger was in every controlled move he made. "Why don't you say whatever it is and get it over with! It couldn't be any worse than this hellish suspense of wondering what's wrong."

"It's about Triple." The remaining color drained from her cheeks. She bit her bottom lip until it bled.

"What about him?" Nick demanded in a tautly edged voice.

Seconds ticked by in silence.

Her frightened eyes met the harsh brilliance of Nick's. There was a hideous expectancy about him. She felt as if she were sitting on the edge of a volcano with an eruption only seconds away. Her world was about to disintegrate.

"I'm not really his mother," she whispered.

Although Nick didn't move, he seemed to loom nearer. "I don't believe you," he rasped. "Next you'll be saying he's not my son."

"H-he's not." Bitter tears of remorse filled her eyes. "Oh, Nick, I thought he was. For years I believed it!"

"You're lying!"

"If only I were. I'm telling the truth."

"No!" he shouted. He grabbed her by the shoulders and began to shake her. Then he seemed to realize what he was doing and let her go.

"Triple is Lorrie and your brother Jack's son, not ours! When she got pregnant, she told me he was your child. I believed her without even asking you. Don't you see—"

"No! I don't see a damned thing!" he thundered.

"Lorrie told me she slept with you that last night you were in L.A. I believed her. That's why I didn't go to Berkeley. That's why I was so cold to you afterward, why I hated you."

"I slept with *you* that last night!"

"But I went to your apartment after that. I saw you with Lorrie. I believed...what I thought I saw. I was so hurt, I hated you so much that I couldn't think straight."

"Your hatred was nothing but a cover for your own guilt."

"No..." She blurted out every horrible detail in a tear-choked voice, and as he listened, his expression took on a deathly calm.

"Why?" he whispered. "Why did you go to Sebastian in the first place and give him the impression you were the one in trouble? Why did you let me believe all these years you were Triple's mother?''

"Because I am his mother in every way that really counts. Because I believed you were his father.''

"The hell you say. That's some stupid excuse you and Lorrie concocted to cover up a coldly calculated plan. Sebastian liked you. He trusted you. He didn't even know Lorrie. You knew Jack was too young and irresponsible to marry. You could never have pulled the wool over my eyes, so you didn't tell me.''

"I *did* believe you were his father—until a few days ago.''

"You set me up to marry you. And you weren't even his mother. For years I've lived with the guilt of what I believed I'd done to you. It killed me every time I thought of you pregnant and alone.'' He laughed bitterly. "Even tonight you let me go on believing all that.''

"I wanted to tell you the truth. Oh, Nick, I wanted to so much. But I didn't want to ruin your parents' visit, and after they left I was too tired.''

"I've done everything in my power to try to make up to you for the wrong I thought I'd done you. You went to Sebastian, took his money, and turned him against me. You let me marry you, knowing—'' He paused. "I remember the way you and Lorrie were so impressed with the moneyed world, how ambitious you were—to make it on your own, you said. Hell! Not when you saw an easier way. You deliberately used Triple, Jack's son, to get your start in the business world. You took money from Sebastian, from me. And Triple's not even yours.''

"I thought I had to go to Sebastian. I had to get the money to take care of Lorrie. There was no one else I could turn to. After Triple was born, I couldn't have loved him more if he'd been my real son. I didn't marry you for your money. I married you because I thought you had a better claim to him than I did. You might have found out I was only his aunt. There was a nurse...who knew the truth. He wasn't even legally mine. You could have taken him.''

The thrust of his frozen gaze pierced her like the coldest blade.

''And when Jack died, why did you come to me then and bind me to you with your warmth and love? You must have seen how vulnerable I was. You knew exactly how to keep me on the hook, loving you, paying... What a fool I've been.''

''It wasn't like that, I swear it. You were so desperate, I was afraid for you that night. I wanted you so much the next morning, I almost told you everything. But I couldn't because I still believed Lorrie.''

''I don't want to hear any more.''

A tiny sob escaped from Amy's lips. She turned away. ''I—I can't blame you.''

Nick reread Triple's note. ''So he found out the truth? How can a child understand any of this if I can't? He's out there somewhere, hurting badly. Jack's son. I've got to find him.''

''I'll help...''

Nick's mouth thinned into a cruel line, all savagery and pride. He stared down at her for a long moment. ''No, thank you, darling,'' he muttered viciously. ''Haven't you already done more than enough for us all?''

''Nick, please... Try to understand.''

He broke his gaze away from the pleading look in her eyes, cutting her out of his world as if she no longer existed.

''I do understand,'' he said coldly. ''That's the problem. You should have told me before. If something happens to Triple because you didn't—''

He let his unfinished statement linger in her mind like a shard of horror.

He turned and was gone.

She had lost him.

Ten

A phone rang in the house, and someone picked it up. Then silence reigned again.

The balcony door was still open. Moonlight whitened the surf that rushed onto the pale crescent of world-famous beach. Amy held her face up to the cold ocean breeze. Her tears felt frozen to her cheeks.

The front door swung open and slammed. She heard Nick's footsteps rushing down the hall toward her, and she sensed the controlled violence in his every movement.

She was still in Triple's room, still sitting in the silent darkness, hugging Triple's stuffed gorilla. She felt numb, paralyzed. She'd been there for hours, worrying about Triple, grieving over Nick, yet knowing she would feel even worse when the paralyzing numbness damming up her most piercing emotions broke.

She hadn't gone to look for Triple because Nick hadn't wanted her to, and because never before had she succeeded in rescuing Triple from one of his adventures. When Triple was ready, Triple rescued himself.

"Amy!"

"In here," she called weakly.

He threw open their bedroom door and slammed it. She heard other doors, opening and being thrown violently shut as he reached for her. Lights flashed on and were extinguished.

"Amy! Damn it! Answer me!"

"I'm in Triple's room!"

She bit her lip. Her hands started to shake again. Why was it that now that she knew the bliss of sharing a life and home with Nick and Triple, she had lost it all? She wanted more than anything else to make Nick happy and all she'd ever done was make him miserable.

The door to Triple's room crashed open.

All she could see of Nick was his golden hair shining in the moonlight, but even before he stepped inside or spoke, she felt the smoldering fury of his presence.

"So you're still here?" His voice was harsh, cold.

Inside she was dying. As he came closer, she searched his face for some sign of his former love for her.

White-gold hair, bronzed skin stretched taut across cheekbones and jawline, the cruel line of his mouth, cold haunted eyes, his slow, tigerlike grace struck her with the powerful force of a blow to the gut.

Gasping, she wanted to close her eyes against the shattering pain in her heart, but his cold gaze locked onto hers and wouldn't let go.

"Triple? D-did you find him?" There was an agonizing tightness in her throat.

"Yes. It wasn't so hard once I got to figuring. There was only one place he could have gone."

So that was the only reason Nick had come to her, she thought.

"Thank God. He's all right, then?"

"He's fine," came Nick's cold, low tone.

She was relieved that her son was safe, but her heart was breaking. Only pride kept her shoulders squared and her head held high.

"Where is he?" she managed.

"In Texas. Somehow he got himself to the airport and stowed away in Dad's jet. Megan just called me back a few minutes ago. She found him in a compartment in the back of the jet. Triple was running away, but now that he's there, it's not as great as he thought it would be. He got scared on the plane. He's homesick. He even cried on the phone."

"He's never been away—except to be with you," Amy said softly.

Her eyes met Nick's pleadingly, and he turned away, as if he were determined to ignore the mute appeal.

"I guess he didn't know how lonely he'd feel until he left," Nick said flatly.

"Only Triple could pull off something so dramatic."

"Oh, I don't know." Nick's cynical gaze swept her. "He comes from a wild bunch. It's in his genes."

"Thank you for telling me where he is. I've been so worried."

"Megan could fly him back, but I think it's important we go after him—together. Megan's flying the jet to pick us up in the morning."

"Together? W-why? I thought you were through with me."

He cursed under his breath, his face taut with suppressed anger. "I could kill you for what you've done, but you're the only mother Triple's ever known."

Hurt and humiliation swelled inside her.

"And I'm the only father he's ever known," Nick continued in the same flat, harsh tone. "We have to make him understand that we love him as much as we ever did."

"You mean, you aren't going to turn your back on Triple?"

His jaw tightened ominously. He lifted his hand. But he only raked it through his golden hair in a weary, defeated gesture. "Damn you, Amy," he muttered. "What kind of man do you take me for? You aren't Triple's biological mother, but you love him with a mother's love. Is it so hard to believe I could feel the same way? For years I thought Triple was my son. Do you think anything you could say or do would ever change my feelings for him? I'm crazy about Triple. No matter what you've done, he'll always be mine. He's even more precious to me now that I know he's part of Jack. I lost my brother. I don't want to lose Triple, and right now he's in Texas feeling confused and alone. I came back for you only because when I told him I was coming, he begged me to bring you, too."

Her heart constricted. So it was really over. Nick wanted Triple, but he'd never want her. She had hurt him too deeply. What she'd done wasn't something that could be easily forgiven or forgotten.

"Go to bed," he said. "I'll spend what's left of the night on the couch."

When the sun came up, Nick came into her bedroom with a cup of coffee. Amy was red eyed and pale from lack of sleep.

"Get dressed." His voice and eyes were as cold as the night before. "Megan will be here in an hour."

Amy didn't dare disobey. She dressed quickly, silently. He didn't stay to watch.

They drove in silence to the airport. Except for greeting Megan briefly before she seated herself in the cockpit, Amy and Nick maintained their tense silence. Nick was always especially nervous on airplanes, but he was more so today. When they took off and the jet careened over the blue Pacific, his tan hands clutched the armrest of his seat. Moisture beaded his brow.

Before she thought better of it, Amy had reached across and touched his hand in reassurance. Abruptly he jerked his hand free from hers, got up, and left her, vanishing into the cockpit to join Megan.

Left alone in the cabin, Amy felt jealous and left out. She knew Nick had known the beautiful Megan for years. As a child when Nick had spent his summers in Texas, Megan had always been there. Her mother had run off first, then later, her father. Her older brother had moved overseas. Megan had been raised on the ranch during that difficult period, and Amy knew Nick had the greatest admiration for her. He had always spoken of her affectionately, saying that she was wild and fun loving, that she'd been the only one on the ranch who ever dared to disobey Jeb.

Amy could hear Nick and Megan talking and laughing together. For once Nick seemed to have found a means of distracting himself from his fear of flying. Nick was snubbing Amy, treating her as though she didn't exist.

Perhaps the beautiful Megan had made him forget her completely.

Amy couldn't endure it.

But she had to.

By the time Nick and Amy got to the ranch it was noon. Amy had never been to Texas and was stunned by the vastness of the open mesquite range spreading out beneath an endless blue sky. A ribbon of blacktop with heat waves

shimmering off it seemed endless, too, as the road mean-
dered into the distance. Amy thought the ranch had a stark,
lonesome beauty unlike anything she'd ever seen before.
They drove for miles, after passing through the front gate,
beneath billowing white clouds, through tangled oak motts,
beside oil wells, and past herds of Santa Gertrudis and An-
gus cattle before reaching the white Big House.

"It doesn't look all that impressive," Nick said coolly,
"but beneath all those cow hooves and cactus thorns and
that dry caked dirt there are millions and millions of bar-
rels of oil. I guess Texas was built on its bigness, brag, and
oil. At least that's what this ranch is founded on, along with
my brother Jeb."

Amy made no comment. She could see that the Jackson
Ranch was a world unto itself, an empire carved out of the
desert land between the Rio Grande and the Gulf of Mex-
ico.

Mercedes greeted them warmly, offered them coffee, and
told them that Triple was at the corral. Kirk MacKay, Megan's brother, was teaching him to ride.

"You mean you've turned Triple loose on a cowboy?"
Amy asked dubiously.

Mercedes's smile was indulgent. "Kirk's our horse-
program manager, and he's no ordinary cowboy."

"Kirk's a former CIA agent," Nick said dryly. "For once
Triple has a competent sitter."

As soon as they could, Nick and Amy left Mercedes. As
they approached the pasture nearest the corral, they saw a
tall, powerfully built, Indian-dark man leading a little boy
on a docile, velvet-brown pony. Except for having the same
green eyes, Kirk bore little resemblance to his red-haired
sister. Megan was all spirit and fire. There was a coiled
tenseness about this silent man, a fierce, indefinable rug-
gedness about him as if there was nothing on earth that

could frighten him—ever again. And yet there was a quiet
gentleness in him when he turned his attention to the horse
and child. When Kirk saw them, he waved in greeting.
Sensing their need to be alone with their child, he cocked his
Stetson in a salute and lifted Triple down from the saddle
before leading the pony back to the barn.

Triple hesitated, looking torn and uncertain. Behind him
a windmill groaned as its blades whirred in the wind. A
mother quail was leading her feathered nestlings in a pa-
rade across the road.

Triple stood in the pasture with the wind ruffling his
golden-brown hair. He hesitated, a tiny figure in a vast
world, and his proud, aloof stance clawed at Amy's heart.

"Triple!" she cried out, her voice choked with emotion.
She opened her arms. Her face was illuminated with a
mother's unmistakable love for her child.

For a long moment Triple held himself rigid, his troubled eyes betraying a heart in turmoil. Then he could hold
back no longer. Suddenly he was running through the dry,
waving grasses. He threw himself into his parents' arms in
his eagerness to see them, having forgotten that they were
the very pair he had run from.

"Triple, why did you run away?" Amy asked gently after a while, tousling his curls and hugging his sturdy little
breathless body as she knelt beside him. Her eyes were filled
with tears of joy.

"I wanted to fly. But then it was awful. I was scared. It
was so bumpy."

Nick smiled grimly. His eyes were brilliant with a keen
understanding. Amy saw his brown hand tighten on Triple's
shoulder. "Son, for anyone with a drop of Jackson blood,
flying's hell."

"Why did you run away?" Amy repeated.

Triple looked from his mother to his father, and the warmth and understanding the child saw in their faces seemed to reassure him.

"I heard you talking to Aunt Lorrie. I didn't think I was your little boy anymore, and maybe you wouldn't love me anymore."

Gently Amy tilted his face up to hers. "I will always love you. Always," she said.

"I don't want Aunt Lorrie for a mother."

Amy's fingers lovingly caressed Triple's cheek. "I will always be your mother." Her gaze swung to Nick, who seemed so uncomfortably silent. "Just as Nick will always be your father."

Triple glanced dubiously toward his father and then back to his mother. "Really?"

"Yes," she whispered fervently. "Nothing will ever change that. Nothing in the past. Nothing in the future. He loves you as much as I do. You are our little boy. You have to believe that."

"And I can live with both of you? All the time? Can everything be the way it was?" Triple's small hand tightened its grip on his mother's fingers pleadingly.

Amy's imploring eyes met Nick's. A small, agonized sound slipped through the constricted muscles of her throat. More than anything she longed to give her child the answer he wanted to hear, but she couldn't.

It was Nick's voice that broke the silence.

"Yes," Nick said. "We'll all be together. All the time."

"Really, Dad?"

"Really." Nick was folding Triple into his arms, and Triple was staring trustingly into his father's eyes.

"Don't lie to him," Amy pleaded desperately. "Please, no more lies."

She couldn't bear to hope, for Triple to hope, if there was no chance. It would be too cruel.

Nick's grim gaze met hers. "Trust me," he whispered softly, ironically.

She gave a swift silent nod, and then got up and left them together. It was very important that Triple know how much Nick wanted him.

Amy hadn't walked far when Triple gave a shriek of pure joy. She whirled and saw that Kirk had returned and was lifting Triple into the saddle again while Nick watched.

Suddenly Nick's gaze riveted itself to the solitary woman standing apart from them.

"Amy!" he shouted, calling her back.

She wanted to run to him, to believe that he'd meant it when he'd promised they would always be together. She wanted to stand with him, to hold his hand, to watch their son as he rode Nugget. Nick's tall, bronzed form blurred through the mist of her intense emotion.

She turned away and began to run from them, blindly, stumbling through the deep grasses. Behind her she could hear the muffled thunder of Nick's heavy boots chasing after her. He caught her just short of the Big House and spun her around in his arms.

"Let me go!" she wept.

"Shut up!" His raspy voice was harsh and angry.

Amy strained to push him away, but he merely tightened his brutal grip. "Don't come after me if you don't want me!"

She licked her dry lips.

A muscle jumped convulsively at the corner of his mouth. Rage glittered in his eyes. "Why the hell did you run?" Nick jerked her onto her tiptoes. "You've been running from me, turning your back on me for years and years. Don't ever do it again." He covered her mouth with his in a savage kiss that betrayed a bewildering mixture of emotions—rage, desire, tenderness.

Amy shuddered away from his touch with a moan, but he pressed his body into hers, and she felt the rigid contours of his taut, male body.

Just as abruptly as he'd seized her, Nick released her. He pushed her beneath the dense shade of a gnarled live oak. Her slender, graceful figure was dwarfed by the immense size of him.

"What do you think you're doing?" Amy demanded, trying to hide her trembling from him.

"We've got to talk." His raspy voice was harsh. His lips were clamped so tightly together that there were white lines beside the edges.

"Y-you shouldn't have lied to Triple about us all being together." Her words seem to tremble uncontrollably. Her eyes were golden and luminous, mute in their appeal.

His expression softened as he cupped her face. She felt his other hand wrap around her throat. To her amazement his hands were shaking.

"I wasn't lying," he said. "Do you really think I could live without you? I've tried that. The one thing I learned was that no matter how much I wanted to forget you, I couldn't crush all the memories. I couldn't block out the smell and the taste and the feel of you. The harder I tried to, the more I wanted you. I want you too badly, still, to give you up."

It had been the same for her.

"I didn't use Triple to get money from you or Sebastian, Nick," she whispered. "I needed the money for Triple, not for myself."

His hands held her face still, and he read the agony in her eyes.

"I believe you," he said quietly at last. "I believe you."

"But can you ever forgive me?" Her low voice throbbed. "What I did was so wrong. My only excuse is that I thought I was protecting my family."

As Amy gazed up at him her pain seemed to reach out and touch him, hurting him as much as it hurt her. Then she buried her face in the hollow of his neck, drawing a deep, shaking breath and closing her eyes.

He groaned. Then he drew her closer, his hands moving over her body caressingly, soothingly. "We've all suffered—you no less than I. I can't blame you. You did what you believed was right. Hating you is like hating part of myself. I've never felt as alone as I felt last night. Losing you, finding you, losing you again. It was unbearable."

"For me as well," she said.

"I told Triple we would legally adopt him. He would be our little boy. Ours alone. Just as he's always been. He couldn't be any more precious if he were my own son." Nick's eyes were shining. "Darling, don't you see, you have given me back something of Jack."

"Do you really think we're going to be...a real family?"

"Yes, darling, I do," he said hoarsely. "That's what I've always wanted and never had—to be at the center of a real family."

He kissed her throat gently and then her lips more passionately.

"We're going to have to find someplace to be alone," she whispered after a long time.

He smiled down at her. "Believe me, darling, that's not too hard in Texas."

It was the second lay day of Antigua Race week, and a lazy stillness pervaded the sultry Caribbean island. In some hotel or thatched hut nestled behind a wall of lush purple bougainvillea and crotons, reggae music was playing. It was a dull, throbbing, repetitious sound that seemed to go on and on, endlessly crooning just as the aqua waves endlessly caressed the sugar-white sand.

The tiny harbor was overcrowded. A multitude of expensive racing yachts from all over the world were jammed side by side and docked. Sebastian's *Marauder*, the sixty-five-foot Swan ketch that Nick was racing in the series, was anchored out in English Harbour, a safe distance from the other yachts that were also anchored in the still green-blue waters of Antigua's Hurricane Hole.

Not a breath of air stirred the protected waters. Amy and Nick were alone on the deck of the gleaming yacht drinking iced drinks, relaxing for the first time after days of hectic racing. Triple had gone ashore to participate in the lay day dinghy races for children. The rest of the crew had gone as well, encouraged by Nick to participate in the sail-bag races, drinking contests, or the lascivious-leg contest. Mercedes and Wayne were ashore, too, ensconced in the lavish splendor of their air-conditioned hotel suite.

"Whoever heard of bringing a child on a honeymoon?" Nick teased, his gaze drifting over his wife like an intimate caress.

Her eyes sparkled. "Some honeymoon. Whoever heard of bringing an entire crew along—as well as your parents."

"We need the crew to race," Nick declared practically.

"That's just the point. We're supposed to be honeymooning. Not racing."

He flashed her a hot, eager look. "Thank you for reminding me," he said, pulling her into his arms.

The glow radiating from his face was warm and intense and Amy basked in its loving light. In the months that had followed their reconciliation, she had never known a more complete and serene happiness.

"I had to race," he murmured. "Sebastian's orders. I couldn't leave you behind. Do you really mind...so much?"

"I really mind," she whispered, drawing his open palm to her lips and kissing his fingers. "All I want...is to be alone with you. When you're racing, you never think of me."

"And when I'm not, I never think of anything else but you." He gathered her close to him in a fierce, possessive embrace, and she reveled in his nearness. His golden head lowered gently to hers, his mouth claiming hers in a passionate kiss that rocked her senses. A wild, hot glory filled her. She didn't mind anything as long as she was with him.

She was breathless when the kiss was over, and the tingling sensation remained as Nick nuzzled his face into her raven black hair, his mouth trailing kisses of fire along the sensitive skin of her throat. A tremor shook him, and she knew he was no more immune to the sensual thrill of their embrace than she was.

"I love you," she said softly.

"I love you, too," he murmured. "Maybe we'd better go below..."

"In a minute. There's a little confession I need to make first. A little something I haven't told you."

"A little something..." He was remembering her last confession all those months ago when Nick had learned their son's true parentage. Nick pulled away and as he studied her suddenly grave face, he grew even more alarmed. "Dear God! Not another secret! Not again."

"Yes."

"What? I thought you'd learned your lesson."

She smiled softly into his startled face. "We're going to have a baby. You and I..."

His fingers lightly touched her cheek. The expression on his dark face was incredulous. "For a minute there..." His brows drew together. "What the hell have you been doing on this boat working as hard as the men?"

"I was just going along with your idea of a honeymoon."

"Not anymore," he pronounced emphatically. "The men can tail the jib sheets without you. You should have told me sooner, sweetheart."

"I'm not made of glass, you know."

"I'm not letting you take any chances. We'll get you a hotel room. No more hot nights on this boat."

"Nick," she protested softly, laughing at him. "I like our hot nights."

"No argument," he insisted arrogantly. "You and our baby are much too precious to risk." His arms encircled her gently, lovingly. "This is the happiest day of my life." Gently he traced the lines of her face with his fingers. "I never dreamed... it could be like this. Our child—a beautiful, black-haired little girl like you."

Amy laughed. "I was sort of hoping for a golden-haired little boy. We could call him Sebastian."

"Sebastian, hell! What's wrong with Nicholas?" Nick bent his head and kissed her—a long, deep kiss. Amy slid her arms around his neck, rising on her tiptoes.

It seemed that their souls met, touched, and came together.

"Darling," he said in an aching murmur against her lips.

Once she had asked him not to call her that ever again.

But that unhappy time was a lifetime away.

The sky above the soft green island and its shimmering, azure waters was iridescent pink and blue. A golden band of sunlight trailed away into infinity.

Nick lifted his wife in his arms and carried her below.

*   *   *   *   *

Read more about the Jackson family in DESTINY'S CHILD—Megan and Jeb's story— coming from Silhouette Desire in October. Don't miss Book II of the CHILDREN OF DESTINY trilogy!

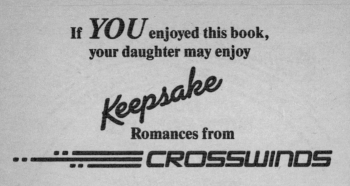

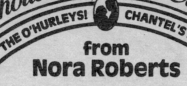

Silhouette Special Edition

THE O'HURLEYS! CHANTEL'S STORY

from
Nora Roberts

Skin Deep

Available September 1988

The third in an exciting new series about the lives and
loves of triplet sisters—

In May's *The Last Honest Woman* (SE #451), Abby
finally met a man she could trust . . . then tried to
deceive him to protect her sons.

In July's *Dance to the Piper* (SE #463), it took some
very fancy footwork to get reserved recording mogul
Reed Valentine dancing to effervescent Maddy's
tune. . . .

In *Skin Deep* (SE #475), find out what kind of heat it
takes to melt the glamorous Chantel's icy heart.
Available in September.

Silhouette Desire

Don't miss the enchanting
TALES OF THE RISING MOON
A Desire trilogy by Joyce Thies

MOON OF THE RAVEN—June (#432)
Conlan Fox was part American Indian and as tough as the
Montana land he rode, but it took fragile yet strong-willed
Kerry Armstrong to make his dreams come true.

REACH FOR THE MOON—August (#444)
It would take a heart of stone for Steven Armstrong to evict
the woman and children living on his land. But when Steven saw Samantha, eviction was the last thing on his mind!

GYPSY MOON—October (#456)
Robert Armstrong met Serena when he returned to his an-
cestral estate in Connecticut. Their fiery temperaments
clashed from the start, but despite himself, Rob was falling under the Gypsy's spell.

𝒟 Silhouette Desire

COMING NEXT MONTH

#451 DESTINY'S CHILD—Ann Major
Book Two of *Children of Destiny*. Ten years ago Jeb Jackson had become Megan MacKay's most hated enemy—but he was still the man she'd never stopped loving.

#452 A MATCH MADE IN HEAVEN—Katherine Granger
Film reviewers Colin Cassidy and Gina Longford were at odds from the moment they met. The sparks between them were dynamite on television and explosive off!

#453 HIDE AND SEEK—Lass Small
When Tate Lambert had uncharacteristically thrown herself at Bill Sawyer, he hadn't been interested. Two months later he had a change of heart, but apparently so had she....

#454 SMOOTH OPERATOR—Helen R. Myers
Camilla Ryland checked into Max Lansing's tropical island resort to get away from it all. But Max was a smooth operator, and he wasn't about to let the beautiful actress "get away" from him.

#455 THE PRINCESS AND THE PEA—Kathleen Korbel
Princess Cassandra led a fairy-tale existence before she met the handsome undercover agent Paul Phillips. He'd rescued her from danger, and now they were fleeing for their lives.

#456 GYPSY MOON—Joyce Thies
The third of three *Tales of the Rising Moon*. Veterinarian Robert Armstrong didn't intend to get involved with a wild gypsy woman. But then he met Serena Danvers and fell under her spell.

AVAILABLE NOW:

#445 PASSION'S CHILD
Ann Major

#446 ISLAND HEAT
Suzanne Forster

#447 RAZZMATAZZ
Patricia Burroughs

#448 TRUE COLORS
Mary Blaney

#449 A TASTE OF HONEY
Jane Gentry

#450 ROUGHNECK
Doreen Owens Malek

Silhouette Desire®

CHILDREN OF DESTINY

A trilogy by Ann Major

Three power-packed tales of irresistible passion and undeniable fate created by Ann Major to wrap your heart in a legacy of love.

PASSION'S CHILD — September

Years ago, Nick Browning nearly destroyed Amy's life, but now that the child of his passion—the child of her heart—was in danger, Nick was the only one she could trust....

DESTINY'S CHILD — October

Cattle baron Jeb Jackson thought he owned everything and everyone on his ranch, but fiery Megan MacKay's destiny was to prove him wrong!

NIGHT CHILD — November

When little Julia Jackson was kidnapped, young Kirk MacKay blamed himself. Twenty years later, he found her . . . and discovered that love could shine through even the darkest of nights.

Don't miss PASSION'S CHILD, DESTINY'S CHILD and NIGHT CHILD, three thrilling Silhouette Desires designed to heat up chilly autumn nights!

SD-445